HER DIRTY ARCHEOLOGISTS

MIKA LANE

HEADLANDS PUBLISHING

GET A FREE BOOK!

Get a free short story!
Join my Insider Group
Exclusive access to private release specials,
giveaways, the opportunity to receive advance
reader copies (ARCs), and other random musings.

COPYRIGHT

ISBN ebook 978-1-948369-78-7
ISBN print 978-1-948369-79-4

Like deals and other cool stuff?
Sign up for my newsletter!

FLEUR HOLMES

"CAMPING? OH, I LOVE CAMPING!"

Never was a bigger lie told. I'd camped once, in my parents' backyard when I was twelve or thirteen, in a tent with my younger sister, Soleil. It didn't go that well.

Sleeping in the backyard is not camping, per se. But I was in a tent, and inside that tent I was in a sleeping bag. On the hard ground. Without my pillow.

So to me, it was pretty damn legit.

Before I had any idea my family was just playing at this camping thing and I realized I could bail at any time and crawl back into the house and my own bed, my mother had said it wouldn't really be camping if I brought a pillow. Pillows weren't 'roughing it.'

Like she was such an expert. If I'd been a little more contrary, I might have told her you also weren't roughing it if there was a flush toilet and a sink for washing your hands ten feet away. But I didn't. I was playing along.

Plus, I wouldn't have put it past her to have my dad fashion some sort of outdoor, rustic toilet for Soleil and me.

All had gone well until the middle of the night. We were sound asleep when the sky split open in an abrupt and ferocious summer thunderstorm. Soleil and I woke, ready to make a dash for the house. We'd had about enough of the camping at that point. But the only thing stopping us was the huge spider in our tent, hanging out on the zipper that closed it. The zipper we had to *unzip* in order to exit. There we were, trapped in a deafening thunderstorm so loud our parents couldn't hear us screaming for help.

Then Soleil threw up. All over the place.

By the time my dad came out to check on us, we'd pretty much lost our shit, having been trapped in a leaking, puke-filled tent with a giant spider taunting us, for god knew how long. Dad dragged us back into the house, the whole time bitching at my mom about her efforts 'to expose the girls to new things,' and especially about having to clean the mess up.

But he didn't clean it. Next morning when the sun came up, I watched Dad from my bedroom window stuff the soggy, puke-y tent, both sleeping bags, and possibly even the huge spider, into the large plastic trash bin out in front of our house. Minutes later, the garbage collectors arrived on my street, erasing the trauma, or at least its physical evidence.

Years later, it looked like my life-long commitment to avoiding camping at all costs might be coming to an end. I'd just started my PhD program in archeology and had to participate in a 'dig,' somewhere in the middle of a North African desert. The thing about archeological sites, is that they don't have Holiday Inns built right next door to them. They're often in the middle of nowhere, which is why there are cool antiquities and such to be uncovered—no one's been digging around there in a long time. Which meant that ten years after my first 'camping' experience, I was about to have my second.

My PhD advisor—essentially my 'boss'—Drake

Bancroft, sat back in his rickety university-issue desk chair, rubbing his chin and frowning as he looked at me.

"You like camping? That's funny. I didn't take you for the 'camping type,' Fleur."

The man was not considered a world-renowned genius for nothing. And the fact that he had my number—or thought he did—had me shifting uneasily in my black suede spike-heeled boots as I stood across his desk from him.

"Oh, Professor Bancroft, are you serious?" I asked breezily, gesturing like I could wave his silly assumption right out of the room. "Camping *rocks*," I said, almost choking on the words.

I was already thinking about what I would wear. A shopping trip was definitely in order. My sister Soleil, now a successful yoga instructor, would know what to get. Her hippy friends camped all the time.

Bancroft's office door blew open and my fellow student Rod whooshed in, brushing past me and grabbing the sole chair in the office.

The one I'd been waiting to have an invitation to sit in.

So I remained standing.

"Hey, Fleur. Hey, Professor B. How's everybody?" he asked cheerfully, waiting for his opportunity to do some major sucking up.

Of Bancroft. Not me.

"Hi, Rob. Come on in," Bancroft said sarcastically.

Rob's oblivious face lit up. "Sure thing, Professor B."

Such. A. Douche.

Bancroft leaned forward, elbows on desk. "Fleur and I were just discussing her joining the dig—"

"Oh yeah, sorry, Prof, that I can't make it. The hepatitis I got on our last trip has still got me down." He patted his stomach.

Confusion washed over Bancroft's face.

But Rob reached up from his seat and patted me on the shoulder. "But lucky for us all, Fleur can go in my place. You have a lot to learn, my friend, but you'll pick it up fast. You're fairly smart."

What?

First of all, Rob was never in the running for this trip.

Second, did he really just say I had a lot to learn?

And third, did he also say I was *fairly* smart?

Delusional, insulting, and condescending, all in the span of less than sixty seconds.

How was that even possible?

Bancroft's eyes darted between the two of us like he was afraid I might smash Rob over the head with one of the priceless artifacts on his bookshelves.

In fact, he popped to his feet, and even though I was pissed to the point where I could barely see straight, I couldn't fail to notice how my professor's dark wash jeans hugged his hips and thighs and other... places.

Down girl.

I wasn't alone in my observations. Female students fought to get into his classes, and rumor had it that some even sat in the front row in short skirts with no panties on.

But the professor had eyes for no one, except his beautiful wife, also an archeologist with the university, her office down the hall.

I'd always imagined what a charmed life they must lead. They were both brilliant, good-looking, well-respected, successfully published, and supportive of each other. They even carpooled to work in their late-model diesel Mercedes and ate lunch together every day.

Well, they *had* done all that. Until recently.

Seemed the missus had found an undergraduate boy toy in one of her classes. And that was the end of the Professors Bancroft love story.

So sad. I mean, who in their right mind would give up a guy like him?

While Bancroft put up a good front, I knew him

well enough to see he was hurting. Regardless, I said nothing.

It was none of my business.

But what *was* my business was my fellow student Rob and his string of nasty little comments.

I pressed my lips together to stop the flow of expletives on the tip of my tongue, and as I realized they might just come flying out of my mouth anyway, Bancroft opened his office door and shooed Rob out.

"See ya later, Professor B," Rob sang, completely ignoring me.

2

FLEUR HOLMES

"I DON'T KNOW WHY YOU PUT UP WITH IT," SOLEIL said, as we picked through the sale rack at Nordstrom.

I held a beige blouse up to my face, but Soleil wrinkled her nose. "That's… not your color."

I stuffed it back on the rack. She was right. It was a bad shade of beige, and it also screamed 'safari girl.'

"Soleil, I *have* to put up with crap from guys like Rob. I can't get into a fight with another student, especially one who has seniority over me. You don't understand how oppressive academic life is. People are just *waiting* for you to trip up. Take one wrong step, and they blackball you so you never get a teaching position or trash your research so you never get published. It's insane."

Soleil nodded sympathetically, but it was clear she really had no idea what I was talking about. Life as a yoga instructor was pretty much all peace, love, and understanding.

But she did look at me with her *'and you're doing this why?'* look.

I ignored her.

"C'mon. Let's go to Victoria's Secret. I need some new underwear. And bras."

Soleil shrugged. "Okay, then. Let's go."

An hour later, loaded down with bags of lacy panties, sheer thongs, and other necessities, we passed my favorite shoe store.

"Oh. My. God," I said.

Soleil's eyes widened when she realized what I'd zeroed in on. "Fleur, are you sure those would work for your trip?"

She looked doubtful.

But I was certain.

In front of us in the window, were a pair of ankle boots with a *wedge heel*.

I headed for the door. "Those babies were made for me. C'mon."

Practical *and* stylish.

Soleil hung back, which was a waste of energy. She knew that once I got an idea in my head, there was no talking me out of it.

"I don't know, Fleur," she said. "Are you sure you can wear wedges in the *desert*? They don't seem very... sturdy."

I shot a look at my sister while I pulled out my credit card. "Soleil. Have you ever been to the desert?"

She screwed up her face as she thought. "Well, no. But I've seen pictures of the desert, you know, in movies and stuff—"

"Mmmm hmmm. Just as I thought. You know not of what you speak."

With that, she shut her mouth and helped me with my bags.

"Hey. Sorry for snapping," I said once we were out of the store.

I was still buzzing from my purchase. The boots were going to be perfect.

I'd been on several 'local digs,' where I only had to drive a few hours from the university. But this one, on the other side of the world in the middle of nowhere, was a different story. I was going to be prepared for anything.

"It's all good. You're the one who's going, not me," she said in a tired voice.

I grabbed her hand. "Let's get a snack. My treat. I have some time before my mani-pedi."

Five minutes later, we were sipping mall milkshakes under the domed ceiling of a food court that smelled like greasy french fries.

I loved this shit.

"So, what did you tell that guy you were dating, you know, about leaving?" Soleil asked. "Is he cool with your being gone for a month or longer?"

Ugh. *That* asshole.

"Oh. Pete. Well, he told me he was going to break things off anyway. Can you believe it?"

To be honest, my thing with Pete wasn't much more than a series of booty calls anyway. No great loss on my part, but of course he had to take the opportunity to tell me he needed to find someone to seriously date since he was finishing up law school. He needed a woman who would make him look good at interviews, and then later at firm functions.

Of course, I told him to go fuck himself, and that I'd be in the desert for a month with the handsome and famous archeologist Drake Bancroft.

And what did he do? He laughed.

"You, Fleur? In the desert? For a month?"

I heard him laughing until he was out of sight.

Things like that happened to me often. Always had. And it made me mad.

People—mainly men—doubted me. They thought I couldn't possibly be smart enough to be in a PhD program. That I couldn't possibly be smart enough to have published research. That I couldn't possibly be smart enough to have been chosen to go on one of the most important archeological explorations in twenty-five years.

And I had all kinds of plans to prove them wrong.

3

DRAKE BANCROFT

"What do you mean your brother and you are joining the dig?"

Jonas nodded patiently.

"You know, Drake, I've been concerned about being out of the game for too long. I need to get my hands dirty again. Get back out in the field."

I did my best to control my rising panic. I had everything for the dig locked and loaded. I had Fleur, my assistant, and two other support staff lined up for the trip.

I had budget for *four* people. Not *six*. There was no room for anyone else.

Even if they were my boss and his brother. My boss, who controlled the archeology department's budget and basically had to approve everything I did.

He patted me on the shoulder as if to offer comfort.

Little good it did.

"You'll have to knock out the two support staff. But don't worry, Drake, my brother Penn and I can carry our own weight. He's a curator and runs ancient acquisitions at the museum. He will be a great person to have along. This could turn into something profitable for the university if he sees something they might be able to use."

For Christ's sake.

"Jonas, this excavation isn't about selling shit and making money. In fact, I can tell you in no uncertain terms, this is not a for-profit endeavor. Nothing's going to be purchased by a museum. Everything will stay with the university's collection."

Fuck if I hadn't had this conversation a dozen times over the years. There was always a delicate balance between the need for research and discovery, and the commercial pressures of funding it. Selling to museums was great and all, but it sucked the passion right out of me. This work wasn't about making fucking profits. It was about understanding ancient civilizations and learning from them.

I tried to push the anger out of my voice. No such luck. "Jonas, I had two support people lined up for this trip. I guess your brother and you will be taking their places?"

Irritation passed over his face that I was still questioning his decision. But that was my job. He might be my boss, but if I didn't push back against bad ideas, what good was I to the department?

"Drake, with my brother and me there, you won't need the support staff."

"Really, Jonas? Who's going to Dig the testing pits? Put up the tents? Make you coffee in the morning?" I snapped.

I couldn't help it. This last-minute revelation was fucking me up. As it was, we had no budget for security for the camp. I didn't like to shoestring my trips —too much to go wrong on the other side of the world in the middle of nowhere.

Jonas headed toward my door. "You know, you could bring someone other than Fleur, if you were really worried about being productive."

At least we were on the same page with regard to *something*.

I thought for a moment. "Yeah. I know. I have some trepidation about that one. But it's time for her to go on a real dig. She's been asking for ages. I can't put her off any longer."

I wanted to put my head in my hands, although I wouldn't do that in front of my boss. But he saw the unmistakable despair written all over my face. The trip was going to shit. I'd get nothing accomplished except for running a summer camp for pampered adults.

"Is that why you're not bringing that other kid you usually take? What was his name? Rob?" Jonas asked.

I nodded. "Yeah, Rob. He got hepatitis on our last trip, so he's not up for it. But he's a pain in the ass anyway. Thinks his shit doesn't stink, and he's honestly not that smart. Fleur can run circles around him."

But could she survive in a desert landscape, worlds away from creature comforts like air conditioning, running water, and Starbucks?

"DRAKE. HOW HAVE YOU BEEN?"

I knew who it was before I even turned around. But I still turned. It would have been rude not to.

Not that I owed my newly ex-wife any more than a modicum of pleasantry aside from what I might offer any stranger on the street.

Funny. You can commit yourself to your life's true love, and one day, it's over. Kaput. Gone. Dead.

That's what it was like. A death.

And the way it happened was so cliché it was more funny than tragic.

I'd been getting some funny looks at department gatherings, though I'd paid them no real attention. Big mistake.

First, there were the staff meetings where my colleagues were avoiding my gaze.

Then there were the whispers at the cocktail parties, which I just chalked up to the usual catty university gossip.

But the last was a notification that spelled it all out for my dumb ass. Someone had slipped a note under my office door.

Thanks for the D, asshole. And by the way, your wife is fucking a sophomore from her archeology 101 class.

And that was the end of my marriage.

The ex hadn't even tried to talk me out of splitting up. From day one, she agreed it was for the best. She'd fallen in love with this kid twelve years her junior, and she appreciated my moving out of the way so they could explore where their passion might lead them.

She'd actually said that.

So, my soul mate, academic partner, and love

moved on. And now, even though the ink on the divorce papers was dry, I was still a little bitter.

"Oh, hey, Amalia," I said, trying not to notice the lush black hair I used to run my fingers through, the bright blue eyes I could stare into for hours, and the lush lips that used to wrap around my—

Stop. Just stop.

She sidled up to me, her books held against her chest like a schoolgirl. That was one of the things I always liked about her. She was fucking brilliant but so unassuming.

Guess I wasn't the only one to find that attractive. Irresistible, even.

"I understand you're about to leave town. How long will you be gone?" she asked pleasantly.

Was she really interested? Or just making polite conversation?

I forced a smile. I wanted her to think I was okay with seeing her, my ex-wife, who'd cheated on me, not to mention crushed my heart on a regular basis at work.

Just your typical divorced couple. Working in the same place.

And I'd always thought that was so cool.

"The dig is a month or so, and then I'll be writing for a couple months. So, no teaching this semester," I said.

She nodded because she knew me so fucking well. "You must be thrilled," she said quietly.

I was.

I looked around the hallway to make sure no one else could hear us. "I am. A whole semester away from my usual undergrads who couldn't give a shit about the course material."

Seriously. Some professors remained unbothered by it, but I found it soul-sucking to spend my days attempting to impart knowledge to a bunch of uninterested kids who were only there to fulfill a credit requirement.

Grad students were more my speed. They could be pains in the ass in their own way, but at least they were there to learn.

"Oh, and hey," I added, "thanks for picking up the slack. I guess I owe you for that."

She'd agreed to take not just one but two of my classes for the semester I'd be gone, which had really helped me out.

It was the least she could do for fucking up my life.

4

_____

DRAKE BANCROFT

HAVE YOU EVER HAD A NIGHTMARE THAT, WHEN YOU woke up, you were totally relieved to know wasn't real?

Yeah, this wasn't one of those times.

I was already wide awake, so the nightmare before me was one there was no waking from. Unfortunately for me.

I'd arrived at the airport early because that's what I did. It was my thing. Part of being organized and in control.

Then Jonas arrived with his brother Penn in tow. I'd never met Penn before.

Jonas hadn't mentioned that his brother was his twin. An identical twin. Like so fucking identical, I didn't know how anyone could ever tell them apart.

Penn and I shook hands.

"Jesus. I didn't know you guys were twins. You look *so* much alike."

They looked at each other and laughed.

Jonas pointed toward the floor. "Damn, Drake, that's some nice luggage you got there. Mine is from Costco crap."

I looked down at the Tumi luggage that had been the last gift from my father before he'd passed.

It was a generous gift, but one I also suspected might cause me some trouble. Just like I didn't wear my Rolex watch around the university setting, I also needed to keep my expensive luggage out of sight.

No one liked a guy who showed off his family money.

I hadn't even wanted my wife to wear her diamond ring around our colleagues. Not that that was an issue any longer.

A lot of academics are one step above broke. No need to throw in their face that I was a lucky son of a bitch who'd never be hurting for money, thanks to my grandfather, the Wall Street financier.

His largesse had allowed me a comfortable life in academics without having to worry about money.

Sure, I could have joined the family business and chased the almighty dollar like my own father had, but that would have made me so miserable I'd have ended up in an early grave.

Penn checked the time on the board displaying departing flights. "Are we all set? Looks like we're boarding soon."

And then she appeared.

Accompanied by someone who looked just as overwhelmed, Fleur, and I supposed a woman who was her sister, had grabbed a luggage cart onto which they piled four giant suitcases, which kept slipping off as they tried to push it.

It didn't help that she was wearing high-heeled platforms and a short skirt that, every time she bent to push a suitcase back on the cart, very nearly exposed her ass.

"Oh. My. God," Jonas said quietly.

Yup.

Welcome to my archeological dig. We weren't even through airport security yet, and I already needed a stiff drink.

"I'll have a tequila, please."

Speaking of stiff drinks.

"Um, it's a long flight, Fleur. You should probably really be drinking water."

She waved her hand at me. "You're so funny. First you thought I couldn't handle my own luggage, now you think I can't handle my liquor."

Well, she couldn't handle her luggage. Why would I think she could handle her liquor?

When she'd finally showed up at the airport, Jonas, Penn, and I rushed to help with the obscene amount of shit she'd packed for the trip, each of us grabbing one suitcase so that the fourth could stay on the cart.

"Hi! This is Soleil," she said cheerfully, introducing her sister to us. "Wow. You guys are serious identical twins," she said to Jonas and Penn.

They looked at each other again.

"Fleur, are you sure you need all this?" I asked.

What could possibly be in all those bags?

Her sister put her hands on her hips. "See, Fleur? I told you this was overkill. You do not need all that shower gel."

"Especially since there will be no shower," I added.

Both women looked at me with the type of horror reserved for people who kill babies.

Fleur spoke first. "Um, wha… what did you say, Professor Bancroft?"

She was trying to hang on to her smile. She really was. But it was melting fast.

Jonas cleared his throat and checked the time. "Yeah, Fleur. There's no shower. But we gotta get a move on."

Still in shock, she said a tearful goodbye to her sister. We helped her check her bags and got through security and onto our plane before the color returned to her face and she got chatty again.

I had to give her credit for resilience. Or at least pretending.

So, yeah, she could handle her own luggage—by getting three strong men to help her.

And now she was ordering another tequila while babbling about some guy who'd just thrown her over because he needed a 'different' kind of woman for the next stage of his life.

I could kind of relate to that, having been dumped myself, although why my wife wanted a nineteen-year-old kid would always baffle me.

After a lousy airline meal was served and Fleur was sufficiently slurring her speech, she reached for her carry-on bag, crammed under the seat in front of her, and began rummaging through it. While she did this, her short skirt crept up higher and higher.

But I was strong. I looked away like the gentleman that I was, but not before appreciating her strong, smooth thighs, and the tiny little blonde hairs that dotted them.

I did not need any more trouble on this goddamn trip than I already had.

Having retrieved a thick paperback, she kicked her bag back under the seat, adjusted her skirt unselfconsciously, and cracked her novel open to about halfway. Relieved that she seemed to be done talking my ear off, I had more time—like I really needed it—to lament the state of my expedition, and wonder how it had gotten so goddamn off track.

And while I was telling myself to buck the hell up, a soft snoring sound welled up from beside me. Not the loud and annoying kind of snore, but more of a light girl-snore.

I had to admit, it was kind of cute.

She'd not made much progress on her book before dozing off, and it had tumbled into her lap. I gently lifted it and found she was reading a romance novel called *Hot Days in the Desert.* On the cover was a bare-chested man in an Indiana Jones-type fedora. Rolling sand dunes in the background.

Is this what she thought our trip was going to be like? If so, she had another think coming.

Something told me not to, but I couldn't help but flip through the book. If the back blurb were anything to go by, it was a story about a damsel in distress kidnapped by unsavory nomads.

And god did I end up regretting my curiosity.

The page where Fleur's bookmark had fallen was an explicit description of the kidnapped woman sucking the dick of one of her captors.

Just when I thought my day couldn't get any worse.

5

FLEUR HOLMES

"What a great flight."

Professor Bancroft, whom I'd snagged a seat next to on the plane, looked at me like I was crazy.

I knew some people were cranky when they had jet lag. But I felt great.

I'd not only finished my super-hot romance novel but also slept a good six hours. I was ready to take on the world.

Even if I weren't going to have a shower for four weeks. Seriously, when Bancroft told me that, I almost fainted. But hey, I was a flexible sort of person. I could deal with anything that came my way.

The flight had been lovely, really, and with all the free alcohol I wanted. Such an awesome bonus for an underpaid grad student like me.

We picked up our luggage and the guys insisted on putting my stuff on a luggage cart for me. I didn't say anything, but I think they were probably showing off a little. It was all good. A little gallantry never hurt anyone.

And Professor Keller's twin brother—what was his name again?—was just as handsome and muscular as he was.

Seriously. It was pretty wild I was traveling with three hunky guys, who also happened to be leaders in the field of archeology. There was nothing better than hot nerds if you asked me.

Not that anything would come of it. But I did plan on enjoying my very own personal eye candy for as long as we were all working together.

After passing through immigration and customs, we burst into the public area of the airport.

Huh.

"Um, Professor Bancroft, does this look right to you?" I asked, stopping short with my luggage cart.

He wheeled his suitcase next to mine and bent closer to hear me over the racket. "What's that,

Fleur? Are you having trouble with your bags again?"

I didn't know why he thought my bags were so out of control.

"Also, Fleur, please call me Drake. We needn't be so formal since we're working together now," he added.

"I... I said... I don't think we're in the right place, Prof—I mean, Drake," I said, swatting at a mosquito.

I looked around the airport at a deafening swarm of humanity. The crowds were so dense I couldn't see the exits, people pushed through the throngs with all their belongings stuffed into plastic trash bags, and every few seconds the crowd parted to make room for guards with gigantic guns. And mean faces.

What sort of hell had we stumbled into?

And more importantly, was it time to turn around and head back home?

"C'mon," Drake yelled over the crowd, gesturing for us to follow.

But the jostling kept me from moving forward any more than a few inches. Thank god he glanced back over his shoulder and saw my distress. He returned to me, threw his own bag on top of all of mine, and began to push my cart.

I wasn't letting him get away from me this time.

And suddenly, there was a hand on my arm. I looked up to find one of the guards smiling down on me.

"American? American girl?" he asked with a gigantic smile.

"Um… um…" I stammered.

But Drake grabbed my arm and yanked me in his direction. "Get off her," he yelled, propelling me into the mass of people.

"What was that all about—" I started to ask, wondering if it was really necessary for him to be so rude.

"You don't want to know. Now, hold my arm," he demanded, extending his elbow while continuing to push our stuff forward, like a fish swimming upstream.

"Where are the Keller brothers?" I shouted above the noise.

He gritted his teeth and moved forward several feet. "Don't worry about them. They'll get through this."

Oh, what had I done?

And how was I going to survive this?

Not only was the chaotic crowd one step away from a stampede, the air was fetid with a humid heat that already had sweat running down my temples and my thighs sticking together. The floor beneath us was uneven and cracked, not at all conducive to my cute platforms, and all sorts of people, animals, and god knew what else were brushing up against and even banging into my bare legs.

I held on to Drake tighter.

Was this all a mistake? Had I studied archeology for years, as an undergrad and now a graduate student, only just now to be learning that places like this were to be a part of my future?

I'd heard the stories. Long days, sleeping in tents, curious locals. But I hadn't expected *this*.

When we finally pushed through open doors into the sunshine, I took a deep breath of relief, only to have my lungs flooded with second hand smoke. Turned out that the airport, chaotic as it was, didn't permit indoor smoking.

Drake stopped and wiped sweat from his brow. "That's always crazy, getting through that gauntlet of humanity. Wow. Fun, huh?" he asked, smiling triumphantly.

Was he fucking kidding?

"Um... yeah. Fun," I said with forced cheerfulness. "That was really... something."

He waved over the crowded sidewalk. "There are the Kellers. Let's go."

With the four of us reunited, I hoped the worst was over. "Okay. What's next?" I asked.

"Well," Professor Keller said, "we have a five-hour bus ride, then we pick up jeeps and drive two hours to the site."

"Wh… why didn't we fly closer to the site, then? And avoid the bus ride."

All three men turned to look at me like I was out of my mind.

Right. Okay. This *was* the closest airport.

"Hey, I'm heading to the men's room before we get on the bus. Anyone else gotta go?" Drake said.

The Keller brothers shook their heads.

"I do. I need to go. Do you know where the ladies' room is?" I asked doubtfully.

"Sure. Follow me," Drake said, extending his elbow once more.

When we reached the bathrooms, Drake brought me right up to the ladies' room door. "Okay. As soon as I'm done, I'll wait for you right here. Don't go anywhere else, okay?"

Jesus. It wasn't like I'd never used a public restroom before. I followed the dirty white tiles, waving flies out of my face.

What a weird bathroom. There were no toilets. But there was one sink. No soap or paper towels, though.

Huh. Must be closed for renovations.

I went back outside and stood exactly where

Drake had left me. And in about one minute, he was back.

"Wow," he said with excitement. "I love the culture shock of when you first arrive in these places. It's so invigorating," he said, taking a deep breath and looking around.

"Oh, um, yeah. But hey, the bathroom seems to be out of service."

He frowned. "Really? What do you mean?"

"Well, there are no toilets."

He looked at me quizzically, scratching his chin. Then realization washed over his face. "Um, Fleur, were there little holes in the ground? Like where a toilet might go?"

I nodded. "Yeah? Was it the same in the men's room?"

"Yes. Fleur, those *are* the toilets. You, um, put one foot on either side of the porcelain, and um, well, squat."

What? How?

That was the most ridiculous thing I'd ever heard.

"They're common in developing countries, Fleur. They say they're actually better for you than sitting on a toilet—"

Whatever. I didn't need to hear anymore. "I can hold it. I'll be fine."

"Are you sure? We may not come across another bathroom for hours.

No. Fucking. Way.

I had no choice. I held my head up and smiled. Which wasn't easy because I really just wanted to double over and cry. "Oh. Okay. Be right back."

I returned to the ladies' room and went into one of the toilet-less stalls. I positioned my feet on either side of the hole, pulled my panties to my knees, and hovered until I'd relieved myself. It wasn't so bad aside from the dread that I might slip and fall into the hole.

I was tempted to just catch a flight right back home. But then I'd have to make my way through the airport crowd again.

I was past the point of no return.

Toilet or not.

"C'MON. WE NEED TO HURRY."

Drake grabbed my arm, and we hustled as fast as I could in my platform shoes toward the bus, which looked all boarded and ready to go.

"Wait," I said, stopping before we climbed on, "where's my stuff? You know, my suitcases?"

Thank god I'd kept my carryon bag with me.

"Jonas and Penn put everything under the bus in storage. We're good to go."

He bounded up the steps of the bus and only turned around when he was at the top. "Are you coming?"

I looked down at the front of my shirt, soaked with perspiration, the mosquito bites on my arms that were starting to really itch, and then back at the airport, humming with more bodies than it was designed to hold. But I knew that on the other side of the throng of people lay at least one or two airlines that could take me right back to the United States in the most civilized manner possible.

There would be smiling flight attendants, real toilets, free movies, and best of all, tequila.

I could make a run for it. Screw my luggage under the bus. There was nothing in there I couldn't live without.

I looked back at Drake, who extended his hand to me while the bus driver gunned the engine as a last warning to move my ass.

I thought of my PhD and why I was doing it. How I would feel when I finally completed all the requirements. How proud my mother and sister would be, sitting in the front row at my graduation, dabbing away their tears.

But the best part would be telling all the doubters

to shove it up their ass. That I made it through an archeological dig in a desert in the middle of bumfuck nowhere.

That didn't even have a shower.

I reached for Drake's hand and climbed aboard.

6

PENN KELLER

"WE'RE HERE? THIS IS THE PLACE?"

I had no idea where my brother Jonas and his colleague Drake got Fleur, and I was betting right about now they were wishing they could send her back. But she wasn't my problem.

I was just enjoying the show.

Since Fleur and her sexy sister had bumbled into the airport, dropping their shit all over the place, trying to figure out where to go, she'd been non-stop entertainment.

I didn't mean to sound like a dick. As if I were

enjoying someone's misfortune, discomfort, or, perhaps, poor decision-making. I wasn't that mean. But the woman was a fish out of water if ever there was one, and her perspective on it all was, well, hilarious.

First, there was her shock at everything. Then, the resignation, where she accepted things as they were, even though they couldn't be more different from anything she'd ever seen in her life. But the best part was her effort to try and act like everything was normal.

When we'd gotten on the bus, there were only a few seats left. Fleur grabbed one, and Drake ended up sitting behind Jonas and me.

"All good?" my brother asked after we settled in and the driver pulled onto the pot-holed version of a third-world freeway.

Fuck me. Five hours of this?

Drake leaned forward and lowered his voice, even though it was unlikely that Fleur, across the aisle from us, could hear over the bus's clanging engine.

"She just experienced her first squatter toilet."

Oh no.

"But I gotta hand it to her," he continued, "she didn't complain. She dealt with it like a champ."

Well, that was something. And while it should

have been the last thing on my mind, I could picture her lifting up that cute little skirt…

Jesus. Get a grip, jerk.

"Glad she survived it. Squatters can be hard to get used to. At least for women," Jonas said.

He'd always been the sensitive twin. Me, not so much.

At the first stop, about an hour into the trip, the woman seated next to Fleur exited the bus. The seat was then filled by a new passenger, a cheerful man missing several teeth, carrying a live chicken in a bag.

The poor bird was squawking and fighting his confinement with violent indignation, which his struggling owner tried to get under control.

To her horror, the bagged bird smacked into Fleur more times than I could keep track of.

This would have been ugly if it wasn't so damn funny.

Fleur had squished into her seat as small as she could make herself, her eyes wide with horror, like the chicken might escape and kill everyone on the bus.

But after a while, the doomed bird settled down, and my frequent checks in Fleur's direction found that she'd dozed off, her head against the bus window. The guys and I quickly followed suit, having been traveling for nearly twenty-four hours at that point.

I'm not going to lie. I dreamt about being at home in my own bed, where it was quiet and cool, where there were no mosquitoes, and where I wasn't pressed body-to-body with other humans who smelled like it might have been a while since they'd showered.

Just when I was imagining turning on air conditioning and enjoy flowing, frigid air, I was jerked out of my sleep by a scream.

From Fleur.

I jumped up from my aisle seat and found Fleur pushing the man next to her out of their row and into the aisle with a combination of her fists, yelling, and kicking him with her high heels.

Those ill-advised shoes had come in handy.

"Fleur! What's going on?" I shouted.

Her neighbor, now fully out of his seat, chicken bag in tow, was frantically trying to escape Fleur's flailing limbs. The bird was screeching again—almost but not quite drowning out Fleur—with the man adding to the commotion with his own bellowing at no one in particular, in a language I couldn't identify.

"He touched me!" she screamed. "Creep! Get the hell away from me."

As if kicking him out of his seat weren't enough, she jumped into the aisle after him as he tried to escape. I stepped aside just in time to avoid being trampled, watching Fleur continue to push and kick until the guy was all the way at the front of the bus. Even though we weren't at a stop, and were clearly in the middle of nowhere, the driver pulled over and opened the door.

Everyone else on the bus was now buzzing, craning their necks to see the uproar.

"That's right, asshole," Fleur yelled. "Get OUT!"

The terrified man ran off the bus before realizing he was in the middle of nowhere. The driver closed the door and hit the gas, slapping his leg and laughing his ass off at the misfortune of his countryman.

Fleur, now wrinkled, dirty, with her hair hanging limply in protest of the heat and humidity, smoothed herself out and returned to her seat, head held high.

Hot damn.

I think I was in love.

7

PENN KELLER

"WELL, LOOK AT THIS PLACE!" FLEUR CHIRPED.

She was fooling no one.

She might *sound* excited, but the panic splashed across her face for about the tenth time in twenty-four hours was unmistakable.

I, on the other hand, was strangely at home. As if this were the work I was *meant* to do. I looked over at my brother, and he nodded back, clearly thinking the same.

There was something exhilarating about traveling on dusty, dirt roads, the desert landscape rolling as far as the eye could see. And, as if it were possible, the excitement multiplied the moment the intended destination came into view. These archeological sites were really nothing more than makeshift little cities, scraped together with the most basic of amenities—barely enough to keep their inhabitants alive for the length of time they'd be excavating.

And alive did not equal comfortable.

We arrived just as the sun was going down, leaving us little time to set up our camp before we lost daylight. But our timing also treated us to the first of many majestic desert sunsets.

Life was good.

But not so much for Fleur.

She'd had the presence of mind to change out of her high heels and mini-skirt before we got into the jeeps carrying us from the closest village to the site. So when she jumped out, her sneakers stirred up a cloud of powdery sand. The hem of her perfectly pressed khaki pants was now coated in desert, another insult to her being.

"C'mon everybody. Let's get the tents up. Then we can move our things in and cook something for dinner," my brother announced.

Jonas mapped out where each of our tents should go, as well as our makeshift mess tent where all the cooking and hanging out would take place, and he,

Drake, and I started setting up, starting with the lab tent where we'd keep our tools and inventory any valuables we found.

Fleur took a seat on the ground and after shaking out the contents of her tent bag, grabbed the accompanying instructions and was trying to read them in the waning light.

"Drake, I'm thinking we ought to help her out?" I suggested quietly.

He glanced her way and responded in a low voice. "Let her work on it. She'll figure it out. Everyone handles their own shit. That's how I run the show."

He was her boss, so I let it go.

In minutes, we guys were not only done pitching our tents but had also moved our belongings into them and were outfitting the makeshift kitchen. Fleur, on the other hand, was still studying her tent diagram, occasionally picking up a tent pole and looking at it like it was a mortal enemy.

So I took matters into my own hands.

Drake might not have wanted me to help, but that was bullshit. Sure, we three guys could get our tents up in a matter of minutes, but that was because we'd done it a hundred times before.

How often had Fleur put up a tent?

From the looks of it, *never.*

"Hey, Fleur."

She looked up from her instructions, and in the early evening light, I could swear her eyes were rimmed with red.

It was time to help the woman out. Drake could go to hell.

I extended my hand and pulled her up off the ground. "Gather up all the poles and move them aside."

As she did, I spread the tent base out and secured two corners with stakes.

"Let's put in these other stakes," I said, waving her over.

If she was going to become an archeologist and frequent excavations, pitching a tent was a basic skill.

"Okay. Push this in as far as you can and finish it off with this mallet," I said, demonstrating.

She gingerly took the stake, then with all the fury bottled up from a shitty day, stabbed the thing into the ground with so much force there were only a few inches left exposed.

"Damn. You're a brute," I teased.

For the first time in pretty much all day, she smiled.

And what a gorgeous smile it was, showing off the pretty freckles on her flawless complexion.

She took the last stake from me. "This is kind of fun," she said, using the mallet like she was killing an enemy.

"Okay. Now I'll show you where the poles go."

She listened attentively as I explained how the poles had interior bungees holding them together, and that after they were extended, she was to slide them through the pockets on the outside of the tent.

I showed her the first one, and she did the rest.

Then, we raised the tent and slipped the pole ends into their clips.

"Wow," she said, hands on hips, admiring her new home. "Hey, what is this for?" she asked, pulling one last piece of fabric from the tent bag.

I took it from her and stuffed it right back in. "That, Fleur, is the rain fly. Helps keep your tent dry. But we don't need this in the desert."

She was beaming. "Sure. Makes total sense. I'm psyched. My tent looks *good*."

On impulse, she threw her arms around me. "Thank you so much, Penn."

I instinctively turned my nose into her thick, red hair and took a deep inhale. While she might have smelled a little different before we'd begun our long journey, even after many hours of sweating in a hot, sticky city, then in the arid desert, she still smelled great—just simple shampoo and a little perspiration.

It had been a while since a woman had thrown her arms around my neck, so in my effort to make it last, I embraced her back and laughed, too, hopefully reassuring her that our embrace was nothing more than a friendly one.

She didn't need to know I'd be jerking off later that night, imagining running my lips down her soft neck...

"Hey, guys," Drake called. "Can you come over for a briefing?"

We all took seats in the camp chairs Drake had set up in our 'kitchen' area. The mess tent was an open overhang consisting of not much more than a gas stove, a few dishes and pots and pans, several large coolers of food, and a week's supply of water, with more to be picked up later from the closest village.

"Good work, everyone," Drake said. "As the field director of the site, I've put together a plan for maximum efficiency. Let me know if you have any questions about it."

My brother would love this, structure being his thing. I preferred things a little more laid back, but I could hang. After all, I wasn't much more than a tag-along on this trip.

Hired muscle, Jonas had kindly told me. But hey,

it was essentially a paid vacation. I wasn't about to look a gift horse in the mouth.

Fleur tentatively raised a finger in the air, her face quite pale in the light of the solar lanterns Drake had set up.

"Fleur, what's up?" he asked.

Her mouth opened and then closed without sound. Finally, she emitted a little squeak.

Jonas leaned closer to her. "Fleur, are you all right?"

Her eyes widened, and she managed to point to the top of one of her work boots. "Is… is that what I think it is? Is that a scorpion?" she asked in a shaking voice.

"Oh. Look at that," my brother said. "Our first scorpion sighting."

"Healthy little critter, isn't he?" Drake said, leaning in for a better look.

My fellow archeologists were clearly oblivious to Fleur's terror. I dashed for a cup to scoop it into before the poor woman had a coronary.

Just as I bent before her to remove the uninvited guest, she put a hand on my arm.

"Wait. Let me."

Really?

She took the cup from my hand and with a deep

breath, held it next to her shoe. Tapping her foot lightly against it, the scorpion clumsily tumbled in.

I reach to take the cup from her. "Here, let me have it."

But she snatched it out of my reach. "I... I've got it," she said, getting to her feet.

We three watched in disbelief as she tiptoed toward the edge of the camp, arm extended to put the maximum distance between herself and the scorpion, and chucked it into the night.

Hot damn. To go from abject terror to balls out fierceness in a matter of minutes? I didn't know many dudes who could do that, much less women. In fact, I'd been on digs before when I'd seen guys run away screaming for less, whether they'd seen a scorpion, a snake, or even a garden variety frog.

"W... wow, Fleur," my brother stammered. "That was impressive."

Impressive didn't begin to describe it.

This woman, completely out of her comfort zone, had just quietly and calmly moved a scorpion from our campsite.

"So what's next on the agenda?" she asked.

8

FLEUR HOLMES

"How'd everybody sleep last night?"

Was he fucking kidding?

Was it okay to want to kill my boss, who had only ever been nice to me and deserved, in large part, credit for guiding me in earning my PhD?

I'd slept no more than two hours, and when I finally did snooze, all I dreamt about were scorpions. Of course. They were everywhere, crawling all over me, inside my sleeping bag, and into my pajamas. All over my face and in my hair.

Just when I was about to die from their poisonous stings, I sat straight up in bed—or should I say on my inflatable camp mattress—dripping with sweat, and struggling to catch my breath.

But I was alive. And it was morning. I'd made it through my first night in a scorpion-filled desert in the middle of fucking nowhere, where I'd be living for a month with no shower.

And there was not a single scorpion in sight, at least not inside my tent.

Only twenty-nine days to go. Give or take.

I slipped into what Soleil called my 'archeology uniform,' of khaki pants and a matching long-sleeve shirt. I'd read that bright colors attracted mosquitoes and flies, but from my experience so far, they were attracted to boring-ass beige clothes, too. Whomever sold me that bill of goods was full of shit.

I lightly sprayed my clothes with super-duper bug repellant, sold to me by the same jerk who claimed khakis kept away the bugs. If the guy was as ill-informed as I suspected, I was in for a world of hurt.

At least I'd gotten all the recommended vaccines —so if I got bitten raw, it wouldn't kill me. Supposedly.

But I had to say, my mood improved considerably when I stepped outside my tent. I never knew desert mornings were so beautiful. The sun was still low in the sky, and the air was cool and still from the night.

The best part was, I was the only one up yet.

Which was good for a couple reasons, not only because I was happy to have the beautiful morning to myself for a few minutes, but it also gave me the chance to try my hand at making some camp coffee, and maybe even toast for everyone.

I knew the guys thought I was a lost cause—totally freaked by my surroundings and in no condition to contribute much of anything to the dig. That they thought I was just here because I had to be and that my future in archeology would be behind a desk.

But their estimation of me was wrong. And they'd be learning that soon.

Hell, I'd disposed of our visiting scorpion the night before.

While waiting for the coffee to brew, I pulled my shoulders back and held my head high as I studied the horizon. That had been one of the most badass things I'd ever done in my life.

Looked like this trip might be full of chances to prove that I could hang as well as any of the guys. It was just that I was still… adjusting.

It was to be expected, if you asked me.

These guys I was with, I was sure their first trip

to a place like this was just as eye-opening. There was no way someone could be prepared for those squatter toilets like I used back at the airport. But hey, I took care of business. And took a picture of that damn thing when I was done so I could show the people back home.

I heard the sound of people in the distance, and realized that at the next camp over—well, the only other camp besides ours—people were getting up and making coffee, just like I was.

Drake had told me that dig, about three hundred yards away, was run by some old colleagues of his, looking for artifacts similar to what we hoped to find.

Like our camp, theirs was mostly guys, and if my eyes weren't deceiving me, a couple of them were staring me down.

Jesus. There weren't many of us women in archeology, but these guys didn't need to act like they were looking at an alien.

Just then, one of them waved. I pretended not to see. I didn't want to encourage him or to think he could come on over for a visit. I had enough on my hands with Drake, Penn, and Jonas.

Seriously. Even when he'd been married, Professor Bancroft was the object of many a college girl's crush. It was easy to see why. The man looked like he'd walked out of a Ralph Lauren ad with his blond, clean-cut looks. And he dressed surprisingly well for a professor. Like, *really* well. I saw the bottom of his shoes one time, and they said 'Ferragamo.' I knew those babies cost mega-bucks.

College professors didn't wear shoes that cost hundreds of dollars, and especially not in the nerd fest that was the archeology department, where most people dressed like slobs. So, there was a little bit of mystery around the man. But I didn't tell anyone what I'd seen. People already talked about him enough, what with his wife making off with some young kid.

The wife he'd clearly *adored*.

So sad.

The buzz around that had been pretty intense. No one could believe his wife would choose some punky sophomore or whatever he was, over the handsome professor. And when he became single, the number of girls who went after his ass were legendary. But he didn't take any of them up on their offers, at least not that I'd ever seen. I worked closely with the man. I was pretty sure I'd know if he were up to something.

Not that it was my business.

Then, there were the brothers. Jonas and Penn.

They'd been blessed by the gods of good looks, just like Bancroft had.

Professor Keller was head of the department where I was studying. He was kind of a big-wig, so I didn't see much of him, burdened as he was with non-academic activities like budgets, hiring and firing, and pressing the flesh with other people like the president of the university.

But when I did see him, well he was one man who could stop you in your tracks. He was probably the tallest man I'd ever seen, usually in a hurry, but when he did have a second to say hi, his glittery eyes would drill into my head and right down to my core, leaving me tingling and a little sweaty.

Rumor had it, Keller was not quite as chaste as Bancroft, and that he might actually have gotten into some trouble by dating a student whose father was a big donor, and that's why he pushed his way into this trip—he needed to lay low for a while. I didn't know why professors messed around with college girls. I mean, did any good ever come of it?

And then there was the second Keller, whose existence I knew nothing about until I arrived at the airport. I casually tried to get the low down on him on the flight over, but Drake was tight lipped, like he didn't even want the brothers there to begin with.

I had kind of wondered why the two undergrads

scheduled to be part of the team had, at the last minute, been uninvited.

So now there were two Kellers to contend with, and hell did that come as a surprise. The universe was in a good mood the day it created those two. Probably still laughing its ass off at what it did to the rest of us.

What were the chances that I'd be camping in the desert with three of the most gorgeous men any woman had ever laid eyes on—and that two of them were freaking identical twins?

Thank goodness, Penn Keller had facial hair. Otherwise, I'd never be able to tell him apart from his brother. They both wore their dark hair on the long side, about shoulder length. Of course, Professor Keller often pulled his back into a pony-tail, which just tempted the girls even more. Penn seemed to mostly wear his down.

Those were the only differences between them, at least that I could see.

"Coffee, *yes.* Oh, you are amazing," someone behind me crooned.

I whirled around to see Professor Keller smiling at me and pointing at the coffee I'd made. And his eyes…

I quickly looked away. I was here in the desert for one reason and one reason only. I did not need to be finding my campmates attractive.

No. That would be completely inappropriate.

"Morning," I chirped, busying myself. "How do you take your coffee, Professor Kell—"

He raised his hands, interrupting me. "Wait, wait, wait. Fleur, please call me Jonas. And my brother is Penn. Okay?"

Okay, I had to look at him now. It would have been rude not to.

And my god, he was cute in his slightly wrinkled clothes and case of bed head. I wanted to just run my fingers through his hair—

Someone else was up, now.

"Morning, bro," he said over his shoulder.

I turned to offer Penn some coffee when my gaze snapped back to Jonas.

There was no telling them apart. At all.

"What happened to your…" I pointed to his face.

Penn rubbed his freshly shaved chin. "Oh yeah. Way too hot for the desert. This will be so much cooler. In fact, if you have any extra elastic, I'll pull my hair back like my brother here. That will be a cooler way to go, as well."

Great. Now, there'd be no telling them apart.

And that's when Drake appeared on the scene, inquiring after everyone's sleep quality. I busied myself pouring coffee and then making more, even though we probably didn't need it, so I could avoid answering his question.

Like I would tell them I'd been up most of the night due in part to my fear of dying from a poisonous scorpion sting.

"You're looking very safari this morning, Fleur," Drake said as I handed him his coffee.

I gestured toward my outfit. Nice of him to notice. "Oh this? I've had these old things forever." I laughed, brushing off what I hoped was a compliment.

"Then why is there an REI tag on the back of your pants?" Penn asked.

Fuck.

"Oh. Isn't that funny, I have no idea where that came from," I lied, reaching around and yanking it off.

"Well, you look great, anyway. Ready to rock that Indiana Jones look, huh? By chance, you don't have a fedora like his, do you?" Drake asked, his eyes crinkling at the corners.

Well, shit.

I actually did have an Indiana Jones-style fedora. But fuck if I were going to wear it now.

I made a mental note to stuff it in the bottom of one of my suitcases first chance I got.

"Thank you for the coffee, Fleur. Since you

hooked us up with this, how 'bout I make breakfast?"

I smiled, still shaking off the embarrassment over my pants—the ones I'd had 'forever.'

"That would be great. I'll just excuse myself for a moment, then."

All the fake enthusiasm was making me sick.

But I was hungry and especially curious to see what one ate for breakfast in the desert. I was pretty sure it wasn't going to be bagels, lox, and cream cheese.

Coffee in hand, I retreated back to my tent to straighten up and hide the unfortunate fedora. And just before my return to breakfast, I hooked my new tool belt around my waist since I was on the first shift along with Drake. I was feeling damn good. Official, even. *Super* official.

I was a real archeologist now.

I just hoped I'd be able to pull my weight while I was learning.

"Holy crap," Jonas said as I clanked around the corner, my hanging tools swinging against each other as I walked. "Now she really looks like Indiana Jones."

Everyone laughed. But me.

I was pretty sure I was being mocked.

"What do you have on there, Fleur?" Penn asked, checking out the collection hanging from my waist.

I looked down as if I'd forgotten what I was wearing. "Oh, you know. My tools—trowels, spades, measuring tape, brushes. I have a sieve and bucket I can attach later if we need it."

I'd found the tools interesting in that they were just little things you could find at any hardware store. I wasn't clear on what was so specialized about them. In fact, the trowels looked just like cake servers. I considered bringing along the one in my own kitchen, from Williams Sonoma, but thought better of it.

"Yeah, that's quite something," Jonas said, rocking that damn crooked smile.

"I need one of those belts," Drake laughed.

They didn't all have them?

I'd found my mine in the back of *Archeology Monthly*, where all sorts of things for the committed archeologist were for sale. It was also where I got my fedora, now mangled in the bottom of one of my suitcases.

"So, um, you guys don't have anything like this to carry your tools in?" I asked carefully.

I was getting the feeling this hadn't been the best purchase.

"I don't have one," Drake boomed, setting hard boiled eggs and canned fruit in front of us.

I didn't really care for canned fruit. Way too

sugary. But I was damned if I were going to open my mouth and ask for fresh fruit.

Drake looked at Penn and Jonas, who shook their heads.

They didn't have them, either?

"But I think I'm gonna get one," Jonas said. "Yours is great. Really very practical."

In spite of his kudos, he looked at his brother and pressed his lips together. Hard.

Fine. They thought I was a dork. I didn't care. Just because they were old pros at this and I didn't know shit, didn't mean I was laughable.

I was going to wear my goddamn tool belt all day, every day, just to show them how useful it was.

9

JONAS KELLER

"Would you like some of my sunscreen?"

Fleur offered me her bottle of something heavily-scented, and most likely higher end than what I had. I shook my head and pulled out the cheap stuff I'd gotten at Target.

"Thanks Fleur. Got my own."

I slathered my arms and the back of my neck, and called it done.

Meanwhile, Fleur was trying to get the sunscreen on her chest without opening her shirt.

I was dying to volunteer to help.

Yeah, I liked women like Fleur. Young, smart, and

eager-to-please. She was totally my type. The only reason I'd never moved on her was that she was in my freaking department. And she was a grad student. Usually, they were too smart to get involved with professors.

Undergrads were another story. They swarmed to their professors like moths to a light. It was unbelievable. I didn't know how half the guys I worked with resisted. A lot of us didn't.

And, on the unfortunate occasion, there was a price to pay for that.

I'd... recently gotten into a little hot water with the university—thus, the reason I elbowed my way into this trip. I needed a little time away.

And as I relaxed back into my camp chair and took in the excavation site, the desert landscape, and the tents I was surrounded by, I wondered why I'd ever become part of the university administration, and left behind the amazing work of archaeology.

I was a fucking idiot, that's why.

This was where I belonged. It was why I'd gotten into archeology. I wanted to get my hands dirty and contribute to the understanding of human history. Who gave a shit about running a department of people?

Drake had the cool job, when it came down to it. Being part of the administration might be prestigious, pay more, and grant me access to other university bigwigs. But it was also mind-numbingly bureaucratic. I was a goddamn paper pusher.

I envied Drake's freedom to take on projects and develop courses.

My brother would have been a better fit for the university. And I'd have been a better fit for the museum, where he currently was.

There'd been a time when we'd both hoped to join the archeology department as academics. But it turned out there was room for only one of us. We competed fair and square, and I'd always felt a little badly I'd gotten the position and not him. But he seemed happy with his museum career. Or happy enough.

But I'd always wondered if we'd each be a little more content if the roles were reversed.

I watched Fleur trot after Drake on their way to the excavation site. It was hot as hell, so she'd changed into some khaki shorts and a black tank top, the type women wear for yoga. That, with her ankle-high desert boots, made for quite the vision. She was a little hottie.

Actually, she was a fucking major hottie. Her wild red hair was now divided into two long braids, swinging down her back, stopping just below the shorts that hugged her ass so nicely. Her thighs were fleshy but firm and jiggled just the tiniest amount when she took big leaps over rocks and other debris on the way to the site.

She turned around at one point and waved, her tits bouncing under her lycra top.

Fucking A. The last thing I needed right now was to lust after yet another college student. I mean, she might be a graduate student, and certainly above the age of consent, but my dick had already gotten me in enough trouble at the university.

But there was just something about this one…

And since restraining myself was just not something I was going to do, especially since I was in my archeologist element, I wandered over to the excavation site where Fleur and Drake were doing some initial surveying.

Penn had gone over to the other camp, to visit with some folks he knew from past trips.

I crouched down next to Fleur, where she had bent to measure something.

"How's it going?" I asked, looking right down her top.

Yeah, I was a dick. There was no denying it.

And her tits were luscious, just like I knew they'd be.

"Ow, shit!" I hollered, jerking my hand back from where I'd rested it on the sand.

"Oh my god. What was that?" Fleur asked, gently brushing the dirt away from the print my hand had left in the sand.

"Wow," she said, pulling something sharp out of the ground. "Someone left behind a knife. Crap. Are you okay?"

I'd wiped my bloody hand down my shirt, hoping to remove as much of the dirt as possible from it, leaving me looking like the victim of a massacre.

"Hey, what's going on?" Drake asked.

"Cut myself. I'll be fine."

I stood to go back to the kitchen area where the first aid box was.

Fleur stood, too. "It's really bleeding. C'mon."

Holding me by the upper arm, she directed me back to the camping chair where I'd been hanging out before I'd decided to chat her up.

And where I should have stayed, minding my own business.

"Before I start, which brother are you?" she asked.

Fuck. I could have fun with this. But I was no longer in the mood.

"Jonas," I said.

Penn strolled back into camp. "Yo. What did you do to yourself?" he asked, looking at the blood down the front of my shirt and dripping from my hand. "Were you attacked by the looters?" he laughed.

I shot him a dirty look. Fortunately, his smart-ass remark went right over Fleur's head. There had been issues with robberies, and we didn't want her to worry. Yet.

"I rested my hand on the ground and this was just under the surface in the sand."

I held up what some idiot from a previous dig had carelessly left behind.

But my attention quickly shifted from my brother and back to Fleur, who was dabbing at my wound with a towel she'd just sprinkled clean water on.

While she played nurse, I had the chance to see her up close. *Very* up close. Her blue eyes were fringed by light eyelashes, nearly lighter than her hair. Her flawless complexion was highlighted by a spray of freckles, and her perfectly symmetrical lips were a deep pink.

And she smelled good. How did anyone smell good in the desert?

I was sorry I'd never paid her much attention. She was beautiful, sure, but even better, her touch was having quite the… impact on me. I wanted more.

And that wasn't a good thing. Right?

At least I kept telling myself that

But now that we were in close proximity, I realized I might have a problem on my hands. Literally.

I pulled out of her grip. "Hey, I think I'm going to be fine. I'm just going to put a bandage on this and call it done." I wrapped the towel she'd been using, now almost completely soaked with blood, around my hand.

She frowned. "Prof—I mean, Jonas, that was a deep cut and with a dirty blade. If you got an infection out here, which is very likely because you know, just look around, this place is about the furthest thing from sterile you'll ever see. You could lose your hand."

Cripes, I knew I had to take care of my hand, but she sounded like it was going to fall off tomorrow.

I started to walk away.

"But Jonas—"

I turned to face her. "I'm fine," I snapped.

Shit. I hadn't meant to do that.

Surprised by my outburst, she studied me for a moment. Then she shrugged. "Fine. Suit yourself," and walked off.

"Jesus, bro. Think you could be a bigger douche?" Penn hissed.

I reached into the first aid kit to finish treating

my hand. "I know. I know. I… have some things on my mind."

Penn got in my face. "Well, don't take them out on her."

"Hey, why don't you not joke about things like looters?" I said.

He nodded. "Yeah. That was a slip. In fact, I was just talking about them with the folks the next camp over. Let me go get Drake. We can discuss them while Fleur is busy."

The three of us took seats in our camp chairs, facing the excavation site so we could keep an eye on Fleur. This was not a conversation she needed to be part of.

"What did you learn?" Drake asked.

Penn shook his head. "The guys over there were hit a couple weeks back."

Fuck me.

"Drake, you said the threat was minimal. That we had nothing to worry about."

He puffed up in his chair. The man had never liked being challenged, which, as his boss, I had every right to do.

"Look, guys," he said, leaning his elbows on his knees, "I have it from a reliable authority that one, what we are going after, they don't want, and two, that the shootout at the last robbery scared the shit out of them. We're fine. Really. They're not coming back."

Having convinced himself, he sat back in his chair, satisfied with himself.

Problem was, he hadn't convinced me. Or my brother.

"And we're keeping this quiet, right? I don't want Fleur to take on any more than she already has," he added.

We nodded. At least there was one thing we agreed on.

I waited until after dinner when everyone was in their tent to go power up the sat phone. I had some contacts who could shed light on the looter problem. I wasn't going to just wait for shit to happen like a sitting duck.

"Hey, what are you doing here?" I asked, having run smack into Fleur. "Still practicing your first aid skills? Thanks for your help, by the way. I appreciate it."

She took a step back, and in the dim light, I could have sworn she looked upset. "Oh. Hey. Just getting something for my fly bites."

She sniffled.

Okay. All was not well. And I knew my behavior probably hadn't make things any better. Time to see if I could redeem myself.

"What's going on, Fleur?"

"Nuthin'."

"I know something's going on. I'm not an idiot. No matter how much I might act like one."

Laughing, she shrugged. "It's just that, you know, there have been some challenges, and these fly bites are really freaking itchy."

Looking down at her feet, she sniffled again, wiping her face with the back of her hand.

"Hey," I said, crooking a finger under her chin. "You're going to be okay. Everyone's first dig is a clusterfuck. You don't know what to expect, and it's all new and overwhelming."

I knew I should have moved my hand off her face, but I didn't.

I couldn't. She'd placed her hand over mine to hold it there.

So, I bent to kiss her, good judgment be damned. We were a long way from home, and if this was the sort of comfort she craved, who was I to deny her?

I knew I shouldn't.

But that didn't stop me from kissing her more deeply. As if anything could.

10

FLEUR HOLMES

I HADN'T MET ANY OF THE PEOPLE IN OUR neighboring camp, but the guys went over there a lot, pow-wowing over something or other. It was no surprise because everyone in archeology knew each other. In fact, I needed to start doing my own networking. But the way one of the guys in the other camp stared at me made my skin crawl. So I stayed put.

Drake had actually been over there all morning, having told me to wait for him, so I was basically sitting around twiddling my thumbs.

Actually, I couldn't complain. Under the tarp

we'd erected over our kitchen area, it was quite pleasant in the shade. And I had loaded my Kindle with new books before I'd left the US, so I was flush with good reading material. All I had to do was choose my next read, since I was done with the paperback Soleil had given me, *Hot Days in the Desert*.

She'd thought it might give me some *ideas*.

But that's not what this trip was about. At least it hadn't been until Jonas kissed me.

It had been nice. No. Actually, it had been great. His lips were full, and he'd kissed me softly at first, and when I didn't resist, he went for it—well, I did, too—our tongues tangled, and he tasted so *good*.

The guy I'd been dating—well, booty-calling with —until right before I left for the dig had actually been a shitty kisser. But he was good-looking and nice enough that I was willing to fuck him on a dozen or so occasions.

He'd kept telling me he liked me, so I figured he wanted more, until he didn't. Which was fine. I wasn't sure I liked him enough to keep him around long-term.

But now, I was surrounded by *men*. Not *boys*. Not stupid college boys who thought they knew everything and could set the world on fire with their newly minted college degrees and no experience under their belts.

My father, when he was alive, had always told me that getting a degree was just the beginning. After that, no matter what the profession, there were still years of learning ahead.

And how right he was. Here I was, about to finish my PhD in archeology, and I didn't even know until today that only a dork bought a leather tool belt from the back of Archeology Monthly. I had a long way to go.

So I might as well make the journey as pleasant as possible, and today that meant sitting in the shade, at least until Drake appeared, watching Penn and Jonas Keller work.

A good gig, if you asked me.

And when I say work, it would be more accurate to call their movement a sort of ballet, that's how beautiful they were. The sweat of their labor poured off their shirtless bodies like it was raining on them. As they moved, first raising their pickaxes, and then bringing them down on the ground with all their strength, they grit their teeth and even occasionally grunted on contact.

The brothers had started the day with a ground penetrating radar machine, a giant thing they'd lugged over in a wheelbarrow that used radar to examine whether anything might be buried in the ground. When they were pretty convinced there was something worth checking out, they cordoned off the area into a square grid, and set to work removing the top layer of dirt.

The gamble was that the machine might sense an ancient artifact, or just a big, boring rock. You didn't know until you muscled the first layer of dirt out of the way, and then got in there with more delicate tools. That's where I would come in.

But until the first layer was cleared, I got to watch the show.

And what a show it was.

So. Freaking. Hot.

Their muscles stretched and contracted over and over, from their rippled abs up to their rocky shoulders, and down their muscular backs.

Every now and then, one of them would stop to push the sweat out of his eyes with his forearm, take a deep breath, and get back to swinging.

"Hey, guys, anyone like some water?" I called, jumping to my feet.

It was the perfect excuse to get closer.

Wonder if Jonas had told his brother we'd kissed.

They looked my way. Guess they hadn't even noticed I was there.

"Um, yeah, sure," one said.

Since Penn had shaved his facial hair, there was no way to tell them apart. I'd hoped they'd at least have tattoos or something that I could identify them by. No such luck.

I filled two canteens with water. I was so excited, I spilled half of one on the ground but finally got the lids on securely and headed over to where they were working.

They'd stopped attacking the earth, having set aside their pickaxes to relax against the side of their trench. One pulled his T-shirt out of his back pocket to wipe off his face, and another took the bandana tied around his neck and put it around his head.

By the time I reached them, my legs were like jelly.

"Um… hi… here… you go," I said, handing each their canteen.

As they chugged the cool water, I stood there, watching rivers of perspiration run down their temples to their chests, their skin deliciously wet and glistening in the sun.

Maybe they needed me to wipe them down?

"Hey, which of you is which?" I asked.

Catching their breath after chugging in one long draw, they looked at each other and laughed.

Cripes, why did they have to smile when they were sweaty and half naked, dammit? As if this weren't already hard enough.

"What do you think?"

Ugh. Of course. They had to turn it into a game.

"You know what? I bet you guys have been doing this all your lives. Testing people. Hell, I'll bet you've even switched before. Fooled a girlfriend or two."

"I plead the fifth. I will not incriminate myself," one of them said.

I rolled my eyes. "Okay, guys. Whatever. See if I bring you water again. And it's awfully hot under the sun here."

More laughing.

"So, before I go back to my very important job of reading in the shade, do you guys need help with anything?"

They shrugged. "We're good."

I grabbed the empty canteens and stomped back to the shade.

I knew what they were thinking. That I had nothing to contribute—aside from being a water runner, that was. In fact, I'd even overheard them talking about me. I'd been returning to my tent after hitting the latrine for a pee late at night.

"Yeah, man, she's good-looking, no doubt. But what is she bringing to the table, work-wise? I mean, she looks like she's afraid to break a nail."

Wrong. That was so wrong.

But here I was in broad daylight, hamstrung from

showing them how I could contribute all because Drake was socializing at another camp.

Fucking A. Why did I have to wait for him to come back, anyway?

And with that, I turned my back to the site, no longer interested in watching the twin Adonises.

I was getting tired of waiting for Drake, as well.

Fuck them all.

11

FLEUR HOLMES

It was the end of a long day of doing pretty much nothing when I went to the kitchen area to fill up my water bottle. But before I rounded the corner, I heard something that made me stop in my tracks.

"Jonas, I'm telling you, the danger is minimal. But if you'd let me hire the guards I'd initially suggested, you'd definitely be sleeping easier at night," Drake said.

Danger? Guards? What the hell?

"I don't know Drake. We're like sitting ducks here. And I worry for Fleur. God knows what could happen to her."

Oh my god. What the hell did that mean?

I didn't move a muscle. I wanted to hear everything.

"Drake, I've told you repeatedly, there was no budget for guards. The department can't pay for stuff like that. The administration would say that if an area isn't safe, then we plain can't go there. It's that simple. So I kept my mouth shut about the risk, on your recommendation."

Okay. That had definitely been Jonas, since he was in charge of things like that.

Long inhale. "We don't have anything to steal, anyway. I mean, we're just surveying the area and creating a grid at this point. There's nothing to come after. Yet." Drake said.

Holy shit. Did they think people were coming to rob us?

Someone got to his feet with a loud yawn. "Well guys, arguing isn't going to solve anything. And I'm tired, sore, and sunburned. Goodnight."

Pretty sure that had been Penn.

When I heard his footsteps, I stepped into the shadows until he passed, then walked into the kitchen as casually as I could.

"Hey there. Just getting some water before bedtime," I said cheerfully.

If they weren't sharing this information with me, there must be a reason. Right?

"Okay, Fleur. Sleep well," Jonas called after me.

Yeah, right. I'd sleep just great after overhearing that conversation.

But as I walked back to my tent, I realized I not only wanted more information, but I deserved it. If there was some sort of danger lurking, who the hell were these guys to decide they could keep it from me?

And what was this danger anyway?

As I walked past Penn's tent, I saw his light was still on. Maybe he'd share some information with me.

"Penn?" I said softly.

He unzipped his tent and poked his head out. "Fleur?"

"Hey, Penn. Do you think we could talk for a sec?"

He held his tent flap open. "Sure. Come in."

I stepped through and took a seat on the end of his sleep mattress. There was nowhere else to sit except the floor, where he grabbed a place opposite me.

"So, I have a couple things to ask you about."

He waited.

I dove in. "I'm going to get right to it. Hope you

don't mind. So… I heard you and your brother saying I was essentially useless. Do you really think that, Penn?"

He sighed then looked down, slowly shaking his head back and forth. Then he looked back up. "I always tell my brother to keep his goddamn big mouth shut. But he never does."

Now it was my turn to wait.

"Look, he's got a bit of a chip on his shoulder about women at the moment. You can't listen to anything he says. He's a good guy and means well but sometimes doesn't think before he speaks."

Easy for him to say.

"Well, it didn't feel good to hear that."

He reached for one of my hands, surprising me. "I can imagine. I'm sorry. I'm sorry we were talking about you. It was wrong."

I gave him a little smile. With him holding my hand, I wasn't sure what else to say.

So I moved on.

"Another thing, Penn. I heard you guys talking about looters."

His eyes widened, and he shook his head again.

"Well, shit."

"Yeah. Well, shit. So, what is this looter talk about? I deserve to know. I'm part of this team just like you and the other guys are."

"You really shouldn't worry about it, Fleur."

Holy fuck. He was going to shut me out, too?

"Penn, I don't want to be afraid the rest of my time here. I need to know what's up."

"You're afraid? That's what's going on?" he asked.

And against my will, my bottom lip began to shake, and my eyes watered until everything was blurry.

Goddammit. I did not want to cry in front of this man.

"C'mon. Here," he said, moving to the edge of the bed next to me and putting his arms around me.

I let my head fall onto his shoulder while he held me.

I had to say, I felt pretty damn safe.

But the tears kept coming.

"I… I'm sorry. I didn't think I was going to get… emotional on you."

He turned my head to face him. "Hey. It's okay. We're a long way from home. We need to support each other."

At that moment, I knew I should look away. The longer I gazed at him, the harder it would be to get to my feet and back to my own tent.

And when he kissed me, it became clear I wasn't leaving anytime soon.

Sure, I'd kissed his brother a couple nights

earlier. But guys did shit like this all the time. Why shouldn't I have my fun?

And any reason to stop flew right out of my mind as Penn ran his fingers through my hair, his hand cupping my ass to bring me closer as he ran his lips down my neck.

Yeah. I wasn't going anywhere anytime soon.

12

DRAKE BANCROFT

I'D JUST SEEN FLEUR'S BARE ASS.

Not what I expected for this trip, but that could be said for the multitude of other things swirling around me.

Everyone else had gone to bed—or so I thought—and I was enjoying my time alone, admiring the full moon shining on the desert landscape. It was times like this that made me love my archeological work.

Actually, I loved digs regardless of the surroundings, whether in the desert or the middle of a busy urban center. There was something exhilarating about bridging past and modern-day societies. I suppose it taught us something about ourselves by taking a look at how humans lived in ancient times and comparing them to how we live now. Why did some societies thrive while others became extinct?

People go into archeology for a variety of reasons. Some just want to travel to exotic parts of the world, while others crave human understanding.

I knew Fleur got into it over something having to do with her father and his death. I'd never heard the full story. Maybe I would on this trip, since we were stuck together for an extended period of time. You tended to get to know your teammates pretty quickly in situations like this.

In fact, sometimes you got to know them better than you really needed to.

It was on a trip like this ten—or was it twelve?—years ago where I met my now-ex-wife.

I'd always been warned not to get involved in any dig-related romances. In fact, someone had even told me that romance put a curse on a dig. I didn't buy that superstition, at least not completely, but hey, our marriage did eventually fall apart, so maybe there was some truth to it.

She'd been in another camp. I'd seen her from a distance the very first day. And after that, I couldn't stop thinking about her. I introduced myself the next day, and we were never apart after that.

Well, until she started carrying on with her new boy toy.

But I wasn't bitter. Not entirely, anyway. I did know, however, that I was off women for a good long time. I just didn't see myself interested in anyone, for any reason, anytime soon.

At least that's what I told myself until I saw Fleur's adorable bottom.

I figured someone in the camp was getting up for water or maybe to use the latrine, when I heard a tent zipper open. I held perfectly still in my camp chair, hoping they wouldn't notice me. The solitude of the night was chilling me the hell out, and I wasn't about to share that with anyone.

As the footsteps got closer, I figured I was about to be discovered. It wasn't the end of the world, and it was high time for me to get some sleep, anyway. But whoever it was took a turn towards the latrine, never noticing me.

Out of curiosity, I craned my neck around the side of the kitchen tent, and who did I see zipping by, but Fleur.

Not that that was some sort of surprise. I mean, everyone has to pee in the middle of the night now and then. But what did surprise me was that she was in nothing more than a long T-shirt—one she probably thought covered her ass, but didn't.

And, she hadn't come from the direction of her own tent.

She'd come from Penn's.

Oh boy. This was *not* good. I didn't deny any consenting adult their god-given right to nookie, but I wasn't a big fan of people hooking up on one of my trips.

The old guy who'd told me romance cursed a dig would be pretty irate right about now, if he were here.

Crap. Old superstitions aside, this could bring a level of drama to my work that I just didn't need. I'd already gotten over the upset of having Jonas invite himself and his brother, thereby edging out the support team I so dearly counted on.

And now I had to keep them calm about threats that marauding looters were on the loose. I wasn't having much success on that front.

Which, I hated to say, may have been for the best, because it was beginning to look like the threat was not only real, but that it was just a matter of time until a robbery attempt occurred. I needed everyone on the team to be on high alert, and ready to protect any artifacts we found.

And I did feel responsible for protecting Fleur. We all did. I realized that sounded sexist, to be extra-concerned about her, but let's face it, in a dangerous situation, a woman is much more vulnerable than a dude.

And besides, we liked her.

Penn especially, it seemed.

Fleur was special. She was smart, driven, and so completely opposite of the more cynical students I advised. She loved the study of archeology. And to top it off, she was beautiful, with her long red hair and full lips.

I'd have been lying if I didn't admit I found her attractive—not in a 'oh, she's pretty sort of way"— but more in an 'I'd like to take her out' way. But hell, she was my advisee. Talk about a conflict of interest.

Plus, I think she'd been seeing someone until recently, as she told me on the plane after several tequilas had loosened her lips. The jerk had apparently dumped her. I could say without a doubt, he'd regret that someday. You just didn't meet women like Fleur all the time. I was glad Penn had moved on her.

Or maybe she'd moved on him?

And now that I'd seen her bare ass, I could confidently say that all the sexiness I'd suspected under her clothing, really did exist.

In fact, when she returned to Penn's tent, I made sure to get an even better look at her ass, her cheeks slightly jiggling as she tried to walk silently in her hiking boots.

Hiking boots and a bare ass. Now, that was a first.

But first things first. I had to address the looter threat.

When Jonas had turned down my budget request for site security, saying there was just no money for it, I'd offered to pay out of my own pocket. After all, I could easily afford it, not that my colleagues knew that. They actually knew nothing about my financial situation, although some whom I'd known a long time might suspect I came from a family of means. My ex-wife knew, of course, but she'd never tell anyone.

My fortune was nobody's business.

But Jonas had shot the idea down, saying the university would never approve it, and I, not wanting to flash my money around, knew not to insist. I'd only offered out of an abundance of caution. Never did I think the threat was truly imminent. But a couple guys with big guns from the local village taking night shifts would have bought us all some nice peace of mind.

So much for that.

The guys in the next camp over, who'd chased off thieves just the week before, had told me looting was on the rise due, in part, to economic uncertainty in the region. When people were desperate for money to feed their families, they did desperate things.

And excavated artifacts can bring in a pretty penny.

On one hand, I didn't blame the thieves. I did, however, blame the rich collectors who created the market for stolen goods.

As I returned to my tent, finally sleepy, I heard the sounds coming from Penn's.

Bastard.

I wouldn't mind being in his shoes right then. Or should I say, between his sheets?

Maybe I should have brought a dude for my assistant, although my PhD advisee, Rob, drove me up a fucking wall.

But I'd brought Fleur, if for no other reason than she needed this trip to satisfy the requirements of her degree. And now that I could hear her little moans and sighs, I was even happier I'd brought her.

She was giving me plenty to imagine when I stroked my cock at night.

13

FLEUR HOLMES

"Good morning."

I stood in the doorway to Drake's huge tent where he sat working at the makeshift desk he'd set up. There were a couple Isaac Asimov and other nerd books scattered on the floor next to it.

I didn't know how he could keep his tent flaps open all day. He'd told me it was for fresh air, but all I could think about were the scorpions that could walk right in.

What if he were stung? We were an hour from the closest village, and probably more than that from real medical care.

As it was, Jonas had a nasty gash on his hand and wouldn't let me near it. Not that I was Florence Nightingale—I just knew that if he didn't keep it clean and protected, he'd be in for a world of hurt. Literally and figuratively.

I just wasn't going to think about it. I could only control what was in my power, and that was to keep my tent sealed up like a vault. Nothing was getting in there. Ever. Except for me.

He pressed his lips together like he always did when I interrupted him. We'd been working together for so long I knew his every facial expression. Although, lately, he'd been more grumpy than usual toward me.

Was it because he thought I wasn't pulling my weight? That I couldn't pick up on what needed to be done?

Doubts raced through my mind, like they pretty much always did when it came to things around school.

So I'd decided to double down, and learn so much so well that he couldn't possibly have a problem with me. As it was, I wasn't getting much work time in the dig, anyway. I mean, I knew Penn and Jonas needed more time to do the actual excavation, but I could get started on something, I'd think. It was like they were protecting me or something, constantly keeping an eye on me, checking in, and making sure I didn't wander off too far.

Not that there was much danger of that. No, I was happy to stay close to the camp. My encounter with my first scorpion was quite enough for the time being, and who the hell knew what was going on with the thieves they'd been preoccupied with, which I wasn't supposed to know about.

"You're done already?" he asked.

I clasped the reports he'd loaned me. In my drive to become indispensable, which started with learning all I could, I'd hit him up for some new resources to study. I'd be that much more valuable to them with an understanding of the ancient painted pottery we were looking for, and when the time came, could even take on writing the first draft of the resulting report.

"Um, yes. They were super informative," I said, smiling broadly.

What I didn't tell him was that I'd been staying up nearly half the night reading everything. Again, to impress him.

Didn't everyone want to impress their boss? Especially when he looked like Drake Bancroft?

He ran his fingers through his hair, normally each strand perfectly in place. But today he was deliciously messy, and his facial scruff from days of not shaving gave him a slight bad boy, I-don't-give-a-fuck look.

To top it off, there was a smudge of dirt on his forehead, his shirt was covered in dust, and there was a tear in the side of his shorts where they'd caught on something.

Such a far cry from the buttoned-up professor who wore Ferragamo shoes.

And it was totally cool. I loved seeing him through this lens, where he was completely in his element.

So sexy.

Not that I should have been thinking about things like that, especially after I'd messed around with Penn the night before. And kissed Jonas just before that.

I guess there was something about the desert air...

No. That was total bullshit. I was surrounded by three gorgeous men, and if they were interested in me, I might want to be interested right back in them. Other people were having fun—why shouldn't I?

Seizing the opportunity to show off, I started babbling.

"I liked how these reports opened by laying out their plan of attack and their expected results, and then summarized their discoveries. The only thing

I'd do different is to add a section for unexpected findings—"

"Fleur, what are you doing right now?" he interrupted.

I looked at the reports in my hand and then around his tent. I'd been about to mention my new understanding of soil discoloration, and its implications.

What did he mean, what am I doing?

"Um, talking to you."

He looked at his watch and got to his feet. "No, what I meant to say was that I need to head to town to pick up some supplies. The guys next door will watch things for us. Do you want to come?"

Oh. Shit. I wasn't so sure about that. I'd heard the local village was teaming with people who chased after visitors until they'd received a hand out.

Not that they didn't deserve a hand out. I just wasn't sure I was up for that.

But he didn't wait for me to answer. "C'mon," he said, pulling on his boots.

I grabbed my purse and followed him out to the Jeep, where Penn and Jonas were already waiting. They nodded their hellos, and I jumped in the front seat with Drake, grateful they both acted like nothing had ever happened between us.

The ride to town was bumpy and dusty, but also

beautiful in a minimalist sort of way. I was beginning to see how people could be fond of the desert. It wasn't a place I planned to spend much time hanging out in, but the appeal was legit.

I rifled through the secret pocket of my purse and pulled out the wad of cash I'd hidden there.

"Holy crap. What are you doing with all that money?" Drake asked, glancing at the pile in my lap.

"Oh, you know, my dad always said to travel with some cash in case something happened."

After I counted my money, I slipped it back into my purse.

Drake shook his head. "You can't carry that much money around in your purse. Put it in your pocket. A buttoned pocket."

I felt my shorts. "I don't have a button pocket. Just these open ones."

He sighed. "All right. Give it to me, then. For safe keeping."

He held out his hand.

So pushy.

"How do I know you'll give it back?" I teased.

Was that tittering in the back seat?

Drake tried not to smile. "Very funny."

His hand remained extended.

"I... I don't know. I mean, I guess I shouldn't

carry this much cash around, but how much safer is it to give it to you?"

I glanced back, where the guys were grinning.

One of the twins extended his hand over the seat. "I'll hold it for you, Fleur. I've got a secret pocket in my pants that my money is in, too. Oh, and I'm Jonas."

Bingo. Red shirt equaled Jonas.

"Thank you. That's very kind. And don't ask me why, but I know I can trust you to safekeep my cash and get it back to me when I'm ready for it. Here you go," I said, handing it over the seat.

"Here's what I want to know," I started, "is there an ATM where I can get some foreign currency?"

Drake side-eyed me again. "What do you need foreign currency for?"

Was he kidding?

"We're heading into town. What if I see something I want to buy in the market? You know, like a souvenir? A gift for my sister?"

"I don't think you'll find anything—" Drake started to say.

But I cut him off. "On the other hand, I do have credit cards. I'll just use them," I said, satisfied with my decision.

More laughter.

These guys were hilarious.

I sighed loudly. "What? What do you know that I don't? Or are you going to make me guess?"

God I was feeling salty.

Penn patted my shoulder from the back seat. "Fleur, if they don't have ATMs, they aren't gonna take credit cards, either."

Oh. Right.

In the distance, a dusty little town drew closer, all low-rise buildings with flat roofs and colorful laundry drying in the hot sun.

"What are we here for, anyway?" I asked.

Drake slowed the Jeep to a crawl as we entered town, and several little kids, who'd been kicking a soccer ball in the street, ran after us. "We need more water and some other provisions."

We pulled into a parking spot, if you could call it that. Drake stopped me before I jumped out.

"Do you have anything valuable in that bag?" he asked, pointing at my purse.

"This thing? Not really. Just my credit cards and lipstick. Stuff like that, since you guys commandeered my cash."

He gestured over his shoulder. "Give Jonas your credit cards, too."

I rolled my eyes. "Really? Is this necessary?"

Jonas held his hand out as the village kids started to surround us.

"Fine, fine. Here," I said, digging them out and putting them in his outstretched hand.

Jeez, did these guys think I was a total idiot?

Turned out there really *was* nothing to buy in the town. So after about fifteen minutes of walking around, seeing the place, and purchasing the items we needed, we grabbed a table outside a café and ordered tea.

Penn leaned over. "See those kids over there? They're checking you out."

I twisted in my seat and waved at them. "They're so cute."

One of Penn's eyebrows rose. "I don't know if cute is the word I'd use."

Seriously?

"Penn, they can't be more than ten or twelve, and for heaven's sake, they're wearing school uniforms," I said, shaking my head.

"Uh, Fleur, I didn't mean checking you out like 'look at the pretty lady.' I meant they're trying to figure out if you have anything to steal."

What the fucking fuck?

"No way."

He shrugged. "Don't believe me. No skin off my back," he said, raising his hands.

I couldn't believe the cynicism of these guys. It was just so sad.

But a minute later, Drake was on his feet, chasing the very kids I'd thought were so cute. It took me a moment to realize it, but the little one had sped by us, grabbed the purse off the back of my chair, and disappeared down an alley with his friends.

"Shit! I really liked that purse," I cried, jumping to my feet and trying to decide whether I should join Drake in the chase.

But that wasn't really an option. He was already out of sight.

Penn grabbed my arm. "Sit back down. There's nothing you can do, now."

"What do you mean? Shouldn't we call the authorities?"

He looked at his brother. Did they have some sort of secret twin language? "It won't do any good. And besides, Jonas has your money, so you're actually fine."

I sank back into my chair. "That's true. But they were just little kids."

Little kids preparing for a life of crime.

"And to them, you are a Westernized rich lady. That's all they saw," Jonas said.

I'd be damned. I was robbed. They hadn't gotten much, but still.

Penn patted me on the back. "Now you can add

this to all the other firsts you've experienced on this trip."

Drake was still nowhere to be found. So, I decided to work it.

"You mean, like kissed two twin brothers?"

The guys looked at each other.

"Well, hopefully that's the highlight," Jonas said, laughing.

"Can I get back to you on that?" I asked.

14

PENN KELLER

"Hey. Hey!"

I turned over in my sleeping bag. Christ, what a strange dream I'd been having. Someone in the distance was screaming for help.

"Get out of here! Get the fuck out of here."

Wait.

This was no dream.

I held perfectly still to see if maybe I were still half-asleep, or if there really were a woman hollering in the distance.

When I heard it again, I bolted out of my sleeping bag and stuffed my feet into my hiking boots. I dashed out of my tent in my boxer shorts, trying to determine what direction the screams had come from.

"Help!" a weak voice was now calling.

Holy hell. It was Fleur.

"Yo, Drake, Jonas, get up!" I hollered as I ran in the direction of Fleur's cries.

I ran past her tent, which was wide open but empty, and then in the direction of the latrine. When I found nothing, I ran over to the excavation site.

"Over here. Please help me," she croaked.

In the dim light, I saw her sprawling on the ground in her nightgown, barefoot and filthy.

She extended a hand toward me. "I think I…"

"What the hell is going on?" Drake hollered as Jonas joined us.

I put my hand under Fleur's head, and slowly lifted her to a sitting position.

"Fleur, what the hell happened? What are you doing out here?" I demanded.

The other guys crouched around her, too.

She put her hand over her eyes and took a deep breath. "Oh my god. I… I heard some noise. I thought it might just be the people from the next camp over, so I got up to investigate," she said in a trembling voice.

"Goddammit, Fleur, you should know better than to do something like that—" Drake growled.

She held her hand up, cutting him off. "I'm not in any shape for a lecture. Thank you," she snapped.

I took her trembling hand. "Then what happened?"

"It was dark and I couldn't see that well, but as I got closer I could see the outline of two men. They were speaking very quietly. I still thought they were from the next camp, just being nosy or something."

People don't snoop around someone else's archeological dig in the middle of the night just because they are curious.

"They were poking around, so I thought I'd ask them what they were up to. When I reached them, they saw me and started to run. But they had something in their hands so I yelled after them. They didn't stop so I started running, too."

She confronted the looters? Jesus Christ.

"Fleur, you need to have your head examined," Drake started to say.

Now it was my turn to hold up my hand. "Let her finish."

"They'd grabbed the piece of that stone tool we were digging out. I tried to take it back from the man. They pushed me and took off. I heard them get in a truck and head that way," she said, pointing.

"Fuckers," Jonas said, shaking his head. "But you're okay, right?"

She started to get up, and then fell right back down, where I caught her. "I thought so, but my ankle. Damn. Guess I twisted it when I fell."

I put her arm around my shoulder and hoisted her up. Jonas took the other side and we helped her back to camp, hobbling to avoid putting weight on the bad side.

"Let's just take her directly to her tent," I said.

While Drake surveyed the site to see if anything else had been damaged or stolen, we set Fleur down on her sleeping bag and propped her ankle up on my lap.

"Shit, Fleur, we don't have ice. This will swell, and it won't feel good. I'll go get some ibuprofen and an Ace bandage from the first aid kit," Jonas said.

When he was gone, I looked at Fleur, her face smudged with dusty sand, her curls sticking up all over the place.

She was beautiful by any measure but something about looking a little worse for the wear was just about killing me. It was one of the biggest freaking turn-ons I'd ever been hit with.

And at the same time, I was overflowing with relief she wasn't hurt worse.

To be honest, my level of relief shocked me. Yeah,

I was attracted to her, and had even already been intimate with her, but I didn't expect to be as worked up as I was.

My urge to protect her was overwhelming. Like, when I thought about the looters potentially hurting her worse than they did, the pure rage I felt toward them made me shake. I'd tear the bastards limb from limb, given the chance.

Never mind that their thievery may have seriously fucked up our dig. That was one thing.

But Fleur's being safe was paramount. I didn't care about anything else.

Jonas returned with his first aid supplies and handed them to me. "Here you go, Penn. If you have everything under control, I'm gonna do a lap with Drake, and then try to get some sleep."

Fleur extended her hand. "Thank you so much for your help. I really appreciate it.

"You're welcome. Next time you hear something suspicious, come get one of us. No freelancing."

He left to join Drake.

Fleur laughed. "I don't know what came over me. At first, I just thought it was one of you guys, but then I thought I'd check. And by the time I realized it was someone who didn't belong there, I just lost my mind and went after them. After having my purse stolen, I guess I was just riled up."

My little badass.

Oh shit. Did I really just say that?

She wasn't 'my' anything.

"As crazy as it sounds, Fleur, I'm kind of impressed. I know a lot of dudes who never would have done that."

She shook her head. "Not sure I set out to confront thieves, but that's how it turned out. Hey, ow!" she cried.

Shit. I knew wrapping her ankle was not exactly going to be pleasant. But I had to say that having her lie back on her makeshift bed with her foot in my lap was kind of hot. Especially since I could see right up her nightgown...

Down boy.

"Sorry, Fleur. But you're good to go now. This will help with some of the swelling, which may help a little in the absence of ice."

Our gazes met, and for a moment, I couldn't look away.

Shit. I was in trouble.

"Hey, do you have any baby wipes? We can get your face cleaned off at least," I said, looking around her tent.

Her hand flew to her face. "Oh shit? I'm dirty? Yeah, they're over there," she said, pointing.

She reached to take the package from me, but I stopped her. "Wait. Let me," I said.

I pulled out a few wipes and leaned close enough to run one, and then another, down her cheek, removing the light-colored dust covering her lovely skin. She turned her face this way and that to make it easier, and when I was done and pulling my hand away, she caught my wrist.

"I think you missed a spot," she said with a naughty smile, turning away from me. She lifted her hair from the back of her neck and bent her head down.

Needless to say, her neck, covered in little tendrils of red hair, was not dirty. I ditched the wipes and leaned closer to run my lips over her warm skin.

When I made contact, she sighed, her body relaxing into mine.

I scrunched her hair into one of my hands. Her neck was nice, but I wanted her lips and I wanted them now. Since the first time we'd kissed, it was nearly all I'd been able to think about. Fuck, half the time I'd been on the dig, I'd been wandering around with a semi-hard on. And it only got worse when I'd finally gotten her naked.

All I wanted to do was hang out in our tents and

ravish her all day long. Like I was about to do, just then.

I knew from the way Drake had looked at me in recent days, that he knew something was up between Fleur and me. Whatever. We were all consenting adults and shit, she neither worked for me, nor was she my student.

I suspected that half of Drake's objection had to do with the fact that he was as smitten with her as I was.

Couldn't blame the man.

And I'd not missed the way my brother Jonas had looked at her, either.

Luckily, I was not a jealous guy.

Taking care not to knock her bad ankle, I lifted up her nightgown to find the perfect pussy I'd explored just a couple nights earlier. She relaxed back onto her makeshift pillow, where she lay smiling, watching me part her legs. Our gazes were locked as I opened her soft folds and ran my tongue through them.

With a sexy moan, she dug her fingers into my hair and gripping my head, pushed me harder into her pussy.

I was so fucking hard I was in pain.

"Oh my god, Penn, yeah, like that," she murmured.

I rested a finger at her opening and slowly prodded until I was inside to my knuckle. I made a 'come here' motion against her walls, and she writhed under me, grinding against my hand until she squeezed and cried out.

I held her as she came down from her orgasm. "Kiss me. I want you to taste yourself," I told her.

She raised her lips to mine. "Yeah, Penn. Let me have some," she said, kissing me greedily.

"I think I'm gonna have to fuck you now, baby," I whispered.

"Yes, Penn. Please," she murmured weakly.

So. Fucking. Hot.

"Hey, guys, I think I know who—"

Startled shitless, Fleur and I looked toward her tent opening to see Drake standing there. With a flashlight in his hand. Looking right at us.

Fuck.

"Ugh, sorry," he mumbled, and started backing out of the tent.

Who the hell left Fleur's tent door unzipped?

"Wait, Drake," Fleur called after him.

Whoa. She was calling him *back*? She had more balls than I'd given her credit for.

After a long moment, he stuck his head back in the tent, this time looking anywhere but at us. "What?" His voice was flat.

Fleur pushed herself up on her elbows, her gorgeous breasts topped by very hard nipples. "Drake. Come join us."

What?

Turned out Drake was just as confused as me.

He turned toward her, taking his time enjoying her nudity and fashioning his response. "Sorry. I didn't catch that."

Good. Very good. Stalling for time.

Smart man.

I needed a second to recover from her bold invitation as well.

And just to make things clear, she extended her hand. "Come here, Drake," she said softly.

Well, if that wasn't hot as fucking shit, I didn't know what was.

My girl wanted to have a threesome.

Actually, I guess I should say *'our* girl.'

Drake stepped into the tent, looking again between Fleur and me. Then he took another step, until he was standing at the edge of the bed, peering right down on Fleur.

I was slightly bummed that I'd been cockblocked by Drake, ready to go as I was. But I also wanted to see how Fleur handled this.

Was she a ménage pro? Or a newbie?

She rolled to her side, and I moved so that I lay

behind her, reaching around to play with her tits. While I did that, Drake dropped to his knees and began to kiss her.

She took his face in her hands. Shit, who knew, maybe they had been together before.

I didn't care. I was only interested in right *now*.

And right now, my situation had gone from hot to fucking scorching.

15

FLEUR HOLMES

"You know how goddamn long I've been wanting to kiss you?"

Yeah. I knew. Or, I'd at least suspected. I'd wanted to kiss him since forever, too.

And when Drake's lips met mine, I was flying. With Penn behind me, pressing his huge hard on against my ass while playing with my breasts, and Drake in front of me, I was sandwiched between the sort of male perfection every woman dreams of. These guys were hot, smart, sexy, and best of all, *nice*.

Who knew nerdy science guys could be so deliciously gorgeous and all about pleasing *me*?

I couldn't ask for more.

Except for the moment to never end.

But I had something else to focus on at that moment, and it was making Penn and Drake feel as good as they were making me feel.

"Drake, I have to tell you something very important," I said.

He pulled back, frowning? "What? Is something wrong?"

Pouting, I nodded. "You have too many clothes on."

He looked at me for a second then dropped his head back and bellowed with laughter.

"Well, shit," he said, climbing to his feet.

His gaze locked on mine, he unbuttoned his dusty camp shirt and let it fall to the floor, revealing rocky pecs and a beautifully flat stomach.

With his boots and socks off, he unbuckled his trousers and after a moment's hesitation, kicked them off. He'd had no underwear on, so now he stood before me naked and perfect.

I hardly knew where to begin, with these two men in my bed. Fortunately, I didn't have to think about it because they took over.

"Penn, you good with all this?" Drake asked.

I looked back over my shoulder and found Penn smiling broadly.

"All good, buddy. I love this sharing... shit."

"Me too," Drake said.

I was glad they loved it. I couldn't say whether I did or not because I'd never done it. But I had a feeling I was going to be a big fan.

"How's the ankle, baby?" Penn asked, positioning me on my knees.

"Better with the ibuprofen, thank god," I said.

Drake kneeled in front of me on the bed, his cock positioned right in front of my lips, while Penn, behind me, rolled on a condom. A second later, he was poised at my opening, where I was wet and ready.

He leaned down next to my ear while Drake slowly stroked himself, occasionally rubbing his cock against my cheek, leaving a trail of his precum.

"Are you ready for me? Are you ready for my cock?" Penn murmured.

Hell yeah, I was fucking ready.

I bobbed my head up and down, no longer able to speak since I'd taken the head of Drake's cock between my lips.

Penn drove inside, filling me to capacity, resting a moment so I could adjust to his girth.

When I started to slightly move my hips, he slid all the way out, then rammed himself back inside.

This pushed me against Drake, who I took as far down my throat as I could.

"Goddamn, you're sexy," he growled, fingers entwined in my hair.

Holding my head as he was, he pumped my face at the same rhythm Penn pumped my pussy. I was sandwiched between two gorgeous men, being fucked on both ends, and I was out of my mind. The pleasure was beyond description, as was the knowledge that I was pleasing them as much as they were pleasing me.

"God, your mouth feels so good, darlin'," Drake growled.

With Penn fucking my pussy, I slipped Drake's cock in and out of my mouth, running my lips along his hard shaft. When I reached the head, I sucked until he groaned with pleasure. His precum was sweet and salty, and I couldn't wait for him to explode in my mouth.

Every inch of me was on fire. I closed my eyes and let myself drown in the touch of the two men.

Behind me, Penn pumped faster, and driving deep one more time, he held himself there, the lengthening and throbbing of his cock setting off my own orgasm.

"Fuck, yeah," he hollered.

My hips bucked as I came, and with one last

drive down my throat, Drake began to spurt into my mouth, grunting and groaning. I swallowed until I couldn't any more, and the last of his cum dripped down my face.

The guys gently lowered my freshly-fucked and spent body onto the bed, where they wrapped me in their limbs until I didn't know whose was whose.

The soreness in my ankle, and the earlier confrontation with thieves, was long forgotten. All I was focused on was how sexy and powerful I felt, and how much I loved archeological digs.

16

FLEUR HOLMES

"Soleil? It's me."

After Jonas had showed me how to use the satellite phone, and I'd promised to keep my call to five minutes, he left me alone so I could have some privacy.

"Oh my god!" my sister screamed from the other side of the planet. "How are you? How is it there? And how are those hot guys? Tell me everything! By the way, you are calling me in the middle of the night."

I laughed. "Okay, Soleil, one thing at a time. First, I only have five minutes to talk. I'm on a satphone, and I they're super expensive. Cell phones don't work in the middle of nowhere, you know."

She let out a loud breath. "Okay. That's why you hadn't returned my text messages. Whew."

I'd told her several times there was no cell coverage in the desert. But that was my sister. Details didn't concern her.

"Soleil, I slept with two of the guys at the same time. And I kissed the third one."

She whooped so loudly I was pretty sure I heard her clear around the globe.

"Jesus, Soleil, you nearly blew my eardrums out."

"Oh my god oh my god. You had a threesome? You little slut!"

Was I a slut? But if I were a slut, then the guys were, too.

"Tell me, how was it?" she breathed.

A tingling shot through my core as I remembered. "It was... fucking incredible."

And I was dying for it to happen again.

Although, maybe I should push that out of my mind. I should not be messing around with anyone I was working with, for heaven's sake, least of all my advisor.

Jesus. What had I been thinking?

Although it had been amazing.

"I'm thinking I made a mistake, Soleil."

She was quiet for a moment. Guess she was all screamed out. "I get it, Fleur. But you're a grown woman. You can enjoy sex with anyone you want."

Easy for her to say.

"Just chill out and enjoy yourself. You deserve a little fun. You've been working on that PhD for years, and you just got rid of jerk-off frat bro—"

"Actually, he got rid of me," I interrupted.

"Whatever. Chill and enjoy yourself. You are with *real* men now. No more piss-ant college boys."

"I gotta go, Soleil. Love you."

"Love you too, sis!"

I packed the phone back in its case and was hobbling back to the camp's kitchen area, which seemed to be the gathering place for us anytime we weren't in our tents or digging away.

"Hey, what happened to your foot?"

I whipped around to find one of the guys from the neighboring camp behind me, looking me up and down like he was hungry and I was a nice, juicy steak.

The guy who'd stared me down from a distance.

And like the guys in my camp, he was shirtless.

Unlike the guys in my camp, his belly hung over his belt, he had man boobs, and he was sunburned.

"Do I know you?" I asked.

While I was hoping that might put him off, he took it as an opportunity to move closer.

He extended his hand. "I'm Brad. It's nice to meet you. I already know the guys here, so I thought I should meet you, too. Since we're neighbors and all."

I shifted the phone case to my other hand and shook his. "Hello. I'm Fleur."

He stood there, looking at me awkwardly.

"Well, I have to go. I need to elevate my foot." I turned to leave.

"Oh wait. What did you do, anyway?" he asked. "To your ankle."

Was it that hard to figure out? "I twisted it."

He took the opportunity to take the satphone from me. "Let me help."

Damn. Now it would be harder to get rid of him.

I hobbled back with him close behind, trying not to put too much weight on the sore ankle.

"Hi, guys. I saw Fleur needed some help, so I came on over," Brad said.

Drake and Jonas looked up from the drill they were trying to fix and frowned.

I knew it was Jonas because Penn had started wearing a bandana around his neck.

"She looks like she's getting okay around to me," Jonas said, turning back to his repair.

I plopped down in one of the camp chairs and

put my foot up on another.

"Thanks for the help, Brad. I'll see you later."

The smile slipped off his face, and he realized he had no reason to stick around. "Okay. Well, I'll see you all later. Take care of that ankle, Fleur. Give me a holler if you need anything. You know, like help. Or want to come over for a beer. We have beer," he said proudly.

"I'll keep that in mind."

As soon as he was out of earshot, Drake looked up at me and winked.

And I almost fell off my damn chair. God, the effect these guys had on me.

"Somebody has the hots for Fleur," Jonas sang.

"Can't blame him," Drake mumbled.

"What? What was that?" Jonas asked.

Drake shrugged. "Nothing."

"Hey, we made you a chair of sorts, Fleur. You can sit in the sand and still do a little work," Drake said.

Oh my god. Here I'd been thinking I was going to be pushed out and possibly even made to go home. Granted, I'd slept with two of the guys and kissed the other, but that didn't mean they wouldn't send me packing the moment I was no longer an asset to them.

If only I hadn't gone after those damn thieves. I'd

been doing so well and now I was hampered by a sore ankle.

Archeology could be a cutthroat business. People didn't like sharing credit if they didn't have to. Not that these guys would do that to me. But you never knew how people would behave when there was a lot on the line.

And Drake believed there was a shitload on the line.

Drake and Penn had left my tent that morning before I was even awake, but Drake had returned, having fashioned a sort of crutch-slash-cane out of an extra tent pole.

"It's crude, but I think it will help. You shouldn't be out of commission long, anyway. That looks like a minor sprain. But I'd be remiss if I didn't ask you if you wanted to leave," he'd said.

"Leave? What do you mean?" I asked, confused.

He gestured at our surroundings. "Leave here. You know, go back home."

My stomach churned at the fear that he might be using my ankle as an opportunity to get rid of me.

Would he really do that? Fuck me over like that?

Especially after he'd fucked me? Literally?

I stood with the help of my new device. "No. Absolutely not. I am going nowhere," I said, my chin held high.

"Are you sure—" he started to ask.

But I cut him off. This wasn't even open for discussion if you asked me. "You can't keep me away from this dig. I'd crawl on my hands and knees to get to it, if I had to."

My voice caught. Shit. I didn't want to look like a crybaby.

"I mean, I usually sit in the same spot for hours, anyway. I'm sure I'll be fine."

He smiled. "I appreciate your dedication."

I appreciated his nice, big dick in my mouth...

And then I started to blush. From the prickling heat all over my face, I knew it was a good one, nice and pink, announcing to the world that I was embarrassed as shit.

"Hey, you feeling okay?" Drake asked, touching my forehead. "You're really red. Maybe it's the heat? Here, let's get you some water."

With the help of my cane, I followed him to the kitchen area, where he propped my foot up and filled a water bottle for me.

I was blown away by his kindness.

And I had a chair to sit in while digging?

You'd better believe I wasn't going home, not until the absolute last minute I had to.

17

JONAS KELLER

"I HEARD YOU GUYS THE OTHER NIGHT."

My brother, Penn, looked up from where he was stirring a pot of boiling pasta for dinner.

He was so busted.

And I had plans to give him plenty of shit.

He rolled his eyes. "If you hadn't heard the three of us, I'd think you had hearing problems," he said with his usual shit-eating grin.

My brother and I might be a couple of the most identical twins anyone had ever seen, but when it came down to it, we were pretty damn different from each other. And yet, we had each other's back with no limitations.

But that doesn't mean I always liked what he did. Or said.

"How'd you enjoy the show, Jonas?" he asked, taunting me. "Or should I say, audio?"

But he wasn't getting under my skin.

I shook my head in disbelief. "It was pretty fucking hot, bro. Her moans and sighs? Some of the sweetest music I'd ever heard."

He nodded. "I know right. I think I've been walking around with a hard on ever since."

We were silent for a moment.

"So, you like her too, huh?" Penn asked.

Fuck if he didn't know me better than I knew himself.

And I couldn't deny it. I had the hots for Fleur, just like any red-blooded man would. She was smart, sexy, beautiful. And one of the things I liked best was her purely guileless view towards life. You almost never came across that in a university setting. People were cynical as hell, clawing their way to the top by stepping on one another.

Fleur didn't operate that way. At least not yet, she didn't. Who knew what sort of toll time would take on her.

And yet I was pretty sure she wasn't the type to

change. She just didn't have the shitiness in her that I saw in some of the people around me.

"Of course I like her, asshole. What do you think?" I snapped.

I poured a jar of pasta sauce over the meat I'd browned. Some of the food at these digs was nasty, but you couldn't really go wrong with spaghetti and meat sauce. Except we ate it so often, I figured I'd eventually come to loathe it.

Penn gave me the thumbs up. "I think you should go for it, then. Test the waters. See if she's interested right back."

"Well shit, if she liked Drake and you, her standards can't be too high," I said, laughing.

Penn rolled his eyes. "Right back at ya, bro."

"Seriously though. I'd noticed her coming and going in the department at school. I mean, how could I not? She's been studying there for a number of years, starting with undergrad. She works hard, gets along with everyone. I just thought it best to stay away from her."

Penn scoffed. "Plus, you were too busy fucking wide-eyed undergrads, anyway."

Well, he got that half right.

"I have had my share of that business. But after the last one, I'm throwing in the towel. Too much trouble, and too much at stake."

Penn knew the story of one of the recent girls I'd made the mistake of getting involved with. Turned out her father was a big donor, and when I started cooling things off with her, she held that right over my head.

I didn't bend to her pressures, which made life a little uncomfortable for a while. The university administration was not happy with me, part of the reason I decided to make myself scarce for a while and join Drake's dig.

Even though he clearly didn't want me. Or my brother.

But I think by this point, Penn and I had proved our worth. The back-breaking work we'd done would take twice as many people and twice as long had Drake brought his usual team.

So it was all good. We'd earned our keep, as well as Drake's respect.

"Hey. How's everybody?"

We turned to find Brad, with a just-opened beer in his hand.

"Hey, Brad. Where's *our* beer?" I asked.

He opened his mouth for a toothy laugh. "Come on over to the camp. Get yourselves some."

I would actually kill for a beer. But alcohol actually wasn't permitted in the region where we were, and while it wasn't hard to smuggle it into one's camp, we'd decided not to risk having our permits revoked over it.

Just wasn't worth it.

But that didn't mean I wasn't dying for one.

"Hey, guys," Brad said, lowering his voice. As he got closer, it became apparent this wasn't his first beer of the day.

Or second or third, actually.

"That girl, Fleur—*fucking* hot. I mean, is she single? I'd really like to get down her pants. See if the carpet matches the drapes, if you know what I mean."

Did he really just say that?

Penn and I looked at each other, and I instantly knew the question bouncing between the two of us.

What to do with this dirt bag...

I was tempted to tell him to watch his fucking mouth, but I could tell from the way my brother was flexing his fists, he wanted to send an even, one might say, *clearer* message.

While we were contemplating our response, Brad was digging himself in even deeper.

He peeked around the corner of the kitchen area to make sure Fleur wasn't nearby.

I almost hoped she was so she could take care of this dirt bag. I had no doubt she could.

"And the tits on her—" he started to say.

Penn had had enough.

He whipped around and grabbed Brad by the front of his shirt. "She's our colleague, asshole. And she's got more going on in her little finger than you do in your whole sorry being. So why don't you hit the road and don't come back until you learn some respect for women."

Holy shit. Penn could be a hothead but I'd never heard him like that before.

But then, I didn't think he'd ever been pushed to anger like that, either.

Brad's eyes were wide with horror. "I... I... sorry, man. You don't have to be so sensitive. Jesus."

Penn let go of his shirt and with a little shove, sent Brad stumbling back a few steps.

When he recovered from his initial shock, anger replaced the humiliation on his face and he puffed himself up to his full height, scowling.

"You guys need to fucking relax a little. Can't you take a joke?" he asked with a weak laugh.

"Brad, I think this is a good time for you to get back to your own camp. We'll see ya later," I said before Penn pummeled him.

He nodded, smiling like nothing had ever happened. "Sure man. And don't forget to come by for that beer."

He waved over his shoulder while he hightailed it out of there.

Penn slammed a pot on our camp stove. "What a dick."

"Who's a dick?" Drake asked, joining us.

"Oh, that Brad dude from the next camp. He was talking shit about Fleur. I almost broke his neck," Penn said. "Told him to get the hell out."

Drake chuckled. "Well. Look at Penn, our badass enforcer."

"You should have seen him," I said. "I thought I might have to intervene."

"Well, hopefully he'll stay away now that you kicked him out," Drake said. "But, hey, I wanted to talk about the looters."

Penn and I both stopped what we were doing. Drake was right, we needed to get ahead of this bullshit.

"I was wondering the same," I said. "They're gonna come back. It's just a matter of time."

"And to be honest, I'm most worried about Fleur. Now that they know we have a young woman in our camp, that's an added attraction for some of these guys. You never know what they'll do," Penn said.

Cripes, he really was smitten.

And he wasn't alone.

Drake peered around the side of the mess tent. "I

didn't want to talk about this at any length in front of Fleur, but guys, we have one gun here in the camp. That's it."

Shit. In most cases, that would have been more than enough.

"It's not only my brother who's smitten with our lovely colleague," I said.

Drake shrugged. "Dude, tell me you're not interested either, and I'll know you're a liar," he said.

I threw my hands up. "You got me."

Drake put his hands on his hips. "Let's agree on this, guys. What happens at the dig, stays at the dig."

I was all for that, especially given the hot water I'd been in as of late with the university. I did not need any more problems. Or drama.

"Speaking of Fleur, let me go get her for dinner," I said.

"Everything will be ready in five minutes," Penn called after me.

"Knock, knock," I said outside Fleur's tent.

I heard some rustling. "What? What time is it?" she said in a sleepy voice.

I unzipped her tent door and popped my head in. "Looks like somebody dozed off?"

She looked around in a slight daze. "I guess so. Geez. What time is it?"

I walked into her tent without waiting for an

invitation. If she booted me out, fine, but if not, I was happy to finally have some one-on-one time with her.

"It's almost dinner time. I was coming to get you."

She thought for a moment. "Oh, thank you. And you know, I'm not even really hungry. But I'll join everyone. Hey, can you grab my shorts over there?"

I reached into a pile of clothes and tossed them to her.

She slipped them on under her sleeping bag and started pushing herself to standing.

"Oh… oh, shit…" she said, beginning to lose her balance.

Perfect opportunity for me to play hero.

I grabbed her hand as she tried to balance on her one good foot.

And I moved closer, of course.

When she looked up at me with her gorgeous eyes and smiled, I took my chance and lowered my lips to hers.

But she pulled her head back abruptly.

"What's wrong?" I asked.

She looked me up and down. "I just realized I don't know whether you're Penn or Jonas. No one wore a bandana today."

Holy shit. That hadn't even occurred to me.

But she must know the difference.

"You've kissed us both now. Yet you can't tell?"

She blushed. "I'm not sure—"

"Oh, hey."

We whipped around to see Penn standing in the tent doorway. "I was just coming to get you guys for dinner."

Dinner could wait.

I planned to have some fun.

"Bro, she doesn't know which of us is which."

Penn's eyes widened. "Holy shit. Really?"

She looked between the two of us as if she might figure it out.

But it wasn't likely she would. Even our own mother had trouble telling us apart unless she could see our torsos.

I had a scar from falling when I was a kid. Penn did not.

"I'll tell ya what," he said. "Kiss me then kiss my brother. Then see if you can tell."

A smile spread across her face. "Okay. I will."

She threw her arms around Penn's neck and pressed her lips to his, while he ran his hands down her hips and clutched her delicious ass.

Then she stepped back. "Okay. Now, you," she said, turning to me.

This time I took her, my hands cupping her

beautiful face. I kissed her deeply, our tongues exploring as she got bolder.

"Okay, okay, you guys. Don't get carried away here," Penn said.

Fleur and I stepped apart, laughing.

"Well?" I said.

She looked between the two of us again. But I could tell from the look on her face, she was no closer to figuring out who was who than she had been two minutes ago.

My brother and I had played this game before. When you're twins like we were, you get a lot of female attention, and that included propositions. And while most of the time we said *no thanks*, there were times we indulged ourselves, and fully enjoyed confusing people.

Our first had been with the girl we'd grown up right next door to. She was older, beautiful, and we'd both had crushes on her since we were old enough to play with our dicks.

She couldn't tell us apart, either.

"I say we try something else to test Fleur," my brother said, looking at me.

We both turned to her. "Any ideas, darlin'?" I asked.

She thought for a moment. "Okay. Yeah, I have an idea."

Damn, the twinkle in her eye was a naughty one. I was already getting hard.

And without any hesitation, she turned to me and began to unbuckle my belt.

Holy shit. This woman was a badass.

She reached inside my trousers and pulled out my now-raging hard on. Running her hands along my shaft, she ran a finger over my cockhead and dragged a little taste of precum to her mouth.

"Mmmm. Tastes good," she whispered.

She turned to my brother and did the same, checking out his cock then lowering herself to her knees and running her tongue across his head.

"So?" I asked, trying to control my impatience.

If she was going to leave me hard like this, I was going to have a field day jacking myself.

But I needn't have worried.

"Gosh," she crooned flirtatiously, "you both taste so good. Different, but both very delicious. I think I might need some more."

Music to my ears.

And dinner be damned.

FLEUR HOLMES

"NOW, WHOSE DICK CAN I SUCK FIRST?"

Holy shit. Did I really just say that?

I was a bona fide slut. Wait till I told Soleil.

Actually, screw that. I wasn't a slut. I was a sexy woman asking for what I wanted. If a dude did that, he'd be a baller.

Why couldn't I be a baller, too?

The two brothers looked at each other like they'd won the jackpot.

Damn right.

I sighed. "Okay, since I can't decide, I will guess. Eenie meenie miney mo…" I paused.

My hand stopped on the cock of the twin on the right. "I'll start with you. Whoever you are."

I dropped to the floor of my tent, favoring my bad ankle, and wrapped my lips around the cockhead before me. Creating a great suction, I pulled back, and Penn or Jonas—who the hell knew?—dropped his head back with a huge groan.

"Fuck me," he growled, digging his fingers into my hair to pull my head closer.

Now that I had his attention, I took his hard cock until he nearly hit the back of my throat, our gazes locked.

There was something about being watched so closely that was beyond intoxicating. And to know his brother was right there, slowly stroking himself, intensified that.

In fact, while the brother I was sucking rocked his hips into my face, I grabbed the other's dick.

I was working them both and it was incredible. There I was, kneeling on the floor of my tent, pussy throbbing without anyone even touching me, and I was pleasuring twins, two identical slices of manly perfection who were focused on me and nothing else, their adoring gazes leaving me wanting to please them as best I could.

Seriously. At that point, they could have asked me to do just about anything and I would have.

But as it was, I was doing a great job bringing each close to his orgasm with one in my mouth and the other in my hand. Each brother rocked toward me, picking up speed, until there was a double explosion, both directed at my breasts, where I rubbed their cum into my skin as fast as it landed on me.

Holyfuckingshit.

Watching each of them orgasm made me dizzy with the gratification that I'd pleased them so well, and that they were happy and satisfied. I wanted to do it again.

When they were done, they collapsed on my camp bed after wiping me down with a towel, each trying to catch his breath. I wriggled between the two and was soon wrapped in four arms and four legs, not knowing where one started and the other ended, still unsure which brother was which.

Penn and Jonas had eventually left my tent, hungry for the spaghetti dinner they'd cooked. But I was too woozy to do anything but lie in my bed, smiling and remembering the guys' faces as they spurted their cum all over me.

The next morning, I was the last to get to breakfast, in part because, with my bad ankle, it took me longer to get ready and then make my way to the mess tent.

"Hey, it's sleeping beauty," Drake said, running a soft hand up my back.

And leaving a trail of goosebumps on my shivering body.

"You guys should have woken me. I hope I didn't keep you waiting."

I looked at the twins and instantly knew which was which.

Penn had gone back to his bandana.

Problem solved.

Now if only I could get them to wear those things when we were in bed.

Yeah, no.

"Morning, Penn. Morning, Jonas," I said.

They each laughed. "Hey, she knows who we are today. Finally," Jonas said.

"I know, man. I was getting a complex. Here I am trying to get to know a woman, and she can't even tell me apart from my also-ran, much less sexually experienced brother," Penn said.

Jonas flipped him off.

We took our seats and Drake served us simple scrambled eggs and sausage patties. I was starving from having missed dinner the night before.

Drake cleared his throat, and everyone looked his way. "Um, Fleur, there is something we all wanted to talk to you about."

Oh. Shit.

I'd done it now.

I'd slept with all three guys, giving them the perfect reason to look down on me, and now they wanted me out.

I could hear it now.

They didn't want a woman like me on their dig.

I was too much of a distraction.

I didn't pull my own weight, anyway, especially with my sore ankle.

So they were sending me home. I'd have to pack up all my shit, someone would drive me to the bus, which I'd have to ride alone to the airport—that dreadful airport—and somehow juggle my numerous suitcases and other things just to get out of the country.

Well, at least this time I'd know not to wear a short skirt and platform shoes. Or the wedge boots I'd been so excited about and which I'd not worn once.

But I'd head home, tail between my legs. Everyone would want to know why I came back early, and if I were even going to bother finishing my PhD.

That about summed it up. I was fucked. Literally and figuratively.

"Fleur, are you listening?" Drake asked, tapping my arm.

I sighed. "Sorry. Got lost in thought. What were you saying?"

Like I needed them to repeat their lame excuses for kicking me to the curb.

But this time I listened.

"We were saying, Fleur, that we were all talking about how much we liked you."

What?

"Um, could you repeat that?" I stammered.

He laughed. "I said... we all like you and are hoping you feel the same."

I looked at Jonas and Penn, who grinned back at me with their perfect smiles.

Was this a joke?

Because, if so, it was *not* funny.

"You... you like... *me?*" I asked, incredulous, looking at them each, one at a time, to assess whether they were bullshitting me.

Penn rolled his eyes. "Christ, Fleur, is that so hard to believe?"

"That we like you?" Jonas added.

Maybe I just needed a moment to absorb it all.

Why shouldn't the guys like me? I was nice, attractive enough, smart, knew how to have a good time.

But *these* three guys, of all the men in the world, all liked me at the same time?

How the hell did that work?

"Well," I said, clapping my hands, somewhat recovered, "I'm glad to know you guys like me. And I like you too!" I said cheerfully.

What else was I supposed to say?

I took a long draw on my coffee and started stuffing my face with eggs. Maybe the guys would realize I was hungry and that later might be a better time to chat.

"It's okay, Fleur. I know it's probably overwhelming to hear that three guys like you at the same time, and that we're all cool with it. But take your time absorbing it, and think about what it means to you," Jonas added.

Um. Okay.

"In fact, we were thinking of taking a trip to the closest town with a nice hotel. You know, for a little break from camping. We could get a suite, swim around in the pool, have a nice dinner. What do you think?" Drake asked.

Now they were singing my tune.

A hotel? With a pool? And a restaurant?

That also meant showers... and air conditioning... and no bugs.

Holy shit, when do we leave?

But I didn't want to seem too eager, lest they think I wasn't in love with camping in the desert without a shower or any other modern amenities.

And having nightmares about scorpions.

Not that living with three amazing men was so bad, when you got down to it.

In fact, that part made it worth the other discomforts.

"That sounds lovely, Drake. What a great idea. It would be fun to get away… and have a break," I said, hoping to hide the fact that I wanted to jump up and down and scream and ask if we could leave *immediately*.

I pushed myself up from the table and grabbed my makeshift cane. "I just have to take care of a couple things in my tent. But leave the breakfast dishes for me. It's my turn to wash."

Jonas rose from the table as well. "Sounds good to me. We have a big day ahead, so I think I'll get started now."

I hobbled away from the guys as fast as I could, my head spinning with the news they'd laid on me.

What the fucking fuck?

Three guys liked me? And hoped I liked them back?

Were they fucking crazy?

Of course I liked them. Jesus. I wasn't an idiot.

But what did it all mean? Surely, this was all just a fling. It couldn't go anywhere.

Could it?

DRAKE BANCROFT

"WOULD YOU JUST LOOK AT THIS PLACE. IT'S incredible."

I pulled the Jeep into the drive at the Hotel Rose, a luxury hotel frequented by heads of state, rock stars, and, well, guys like me. Places like this in the middle of pretty much nowhere were constructed for exactly that reason—because being in the middle of nowhere guarantees privacy for people who rarely have it.

Neither Penn, Jonas, nor Fleur had any idea how much this place cost. And if I could help it, they'd never find out.

I sprang for it because one, I could afford it, and two, I figured we all needed a mini-break from the dig, and speaking for myself, I could rough it for only so long. I loved what I did, no question, but I also treated myself every now and then, too.

I was discrete about it, though. The last thing I wanted was for anyone to think I was a prima donna or, even worse, loaded. I kept that shit under wraps.

I handed my keys over to the valet, and the bellman rushed to get our things. Because we were in the penthouse suite, we didn't have to mess with mundane things like checking in or getting keys. The hotel was ready and waiting for us. They wanted us to feel like we were arriving at our own home.

I was all over that.

Unfortunately, it was only for one night. But hey, I'd be back, and with a little luck, I'd have the lovely Fleur with me.

Not that I was selfish. If Penn and Jonas wanted to join, I was fine with that, too.

I knew we'd thrown Fleur off by telling her we were into her. She had no idea what that meant. Hell, we didn't really know either. We just knew we had to be honest with her. If she wasn't down with hanging out with us, that would be fine. We'd respect whatever decisions she made. She was a strong, independent woman, and we trusted her choices.

We followed the hotel manager into the suite, where he pointed out everything we could possibly need, and most importantly, a terrace with our own private pool surrounded by palm trees and sweet-smelling flowers. How they kept plantings like these alive in the desert was a feat of gardening beyond me.

Last, the good man popped open a bottle of contraband champagne, and left us alone.

"This is insane," Fleur breathed, running through the suite, opening and closing doors. "Broke grad students don't stay in places like this," she laughed.

Her delight told me I'd done the right thing. I could barely keep my eyes off her as she excitedly checked things out in her short dress, almost exposing her ass cheeks every time she bent over.

After a couple weeks of wearing dusty boots, shorts, and T-shirts, when she'd emerged from her tent that morning on our way out, I'd nearly had a heart attack. I'd forgotten how fucking cute she was in her regular clothes, impractical though they may be.

Penn took a sip of the very expensive French bubbles, courtesy of the hotel. "Where'd this come from? I thought alcohol was banned."

"Well, it is. But places like this always seem to find a way to make it available," I said. "I suspect they bribe the local officials, and keep quite a healthy wine cellar to please their high-end guests."

Money enabled all sorts of rules to be broken.

I followed the guys, grinning ear to ear over their luxurious digs, out to the terrace where Fleur had already kicked off her shoes and was dipping a toe in the water.

She squinted toward us in the bright sun. "Anybody for a swim?" she called.

Shit, I'd been dying for one since I'd arrived in this hot, dusty place. And I wasn't waiting a moment longer.

I pulled off my boots, stripped off my sweaty T-shirt, kicked my shorts and boxers to the ground, and with a running start, dove into the pool.

And goddamn if it wasn't a little bit of heaven.

I popped back up in time to see Penn and Jonas dropping trou and following my lead. Once they were in, I spun around to see Fleur standing at the end of the pool with her eyes wide, as if she wasn't sure where to look.

Guess it wasn't every day that a woman got to swim with three naked men.

"You coming?" I called to her.

Her initial surprise faded, replaced by a playful,

devilish one. She yanked her little dress over her head, dropped her bra and panties, and entered like a cannonball, splashing water out of the pool in a big wave.

"Oh my god," she shrieked when she came to the surface. "This is freaking amazing."

She dove back under like a dolphin, her cute little ass cheeks flexing as she pointed her toes.

"Fuck me," Jonas groaned as he watched her surface, then dive again.

I felt the same way, which surprised me. After my wife had made off with her student, I really didn't expect to be attracted to another woman for a long time—if ever. I know I thought I'd never trust another woman.

Was I past all that? I seriously doubted it. But I might be on the way.

Like Fleur, I dove under the water, swimming the length of the pool until I reached her.

"Hey," I said, grabbing her ass and wrapping her legs around my waist. "Having fun?" I asked quietly.

She beamed. "You know I am. This is heaven. Pure heaven."

She leaned back in my arms, the ends of her hair floating in the water like a mermaid's.

I maneuvered us to the side of the pool where I hoisted her up onto the edge, stomach down, so she was bent at a ninety-degree angle over the edge of the pool.

She giggled. "What are you doing?"

"What do you think?" I asked, waving over Penn and Jonas.

In this position, we had a perfect view of her ass, and when I parted her legs slightly, her pussy opened like a delicious invitation.

"I'll let one of you guys do the honors," I said, moving aside.

"What a sight," Jonas growled.

Penn edged his brother out of the way. He reached around one of Fleur's legs for her clit and then buried his face between her legs.

"Oh god," Fleur gasped, arching her back to push further against Penn.

He ran his tongue up and down her puffy folds then pulled back and parted them slightly with his fingers.

Fucking beautiful pussy. I found myself wishing it were right in front of my face, but I'd have my turn. I was a patient man.

Penn inched a finger inside her, quickly followed by another. With one hand working her clit, he finger-fucked her with the other, his face covered in blissful concentration.

"Oh, yes," Fleur murmured, "more like that

please. Oh please…"

"Yeah, baby," Penn said, "squeeze my fingers with that tight pussy. C'mon."

Penn moved faster, ramming his fingers into her pussy again and again, until she screamed in an orgasm.

"I… I'm coming," she said between gasps. "Oh fuck, I'm coming now…"

"Damn," Jonas said to me quietly, shaking his head. "

I jumped out of the pool and helped Fleur sit up. "You good, darlin'?" I asked.

She smiled up at me and let her head fall against my chest. "Mmmm…" was all she could manage, trying to walk on wobbly legs.

"You ready for more?" Jonas asked.

"Fuck yeah," she said, laughing.

The two of us walked her to one of the terrace's lounge chairs. I took a seat, then nestled Fleur between my legs, her back resting against my chest, her ass perched on the very edge of the chair.

Jonas wasted no time in pulling on a condom. "Hold her legs, dude," he said, pushing her knees apart.

Fleur moaned loudly as he entered her, and I imagined my own cock in there, pushing her open and feeling her heat.

With her ass on the edge of the chair, and my arms holding her legs open, Jonas drove into her hard and fast until she began to pound her fists and buck her head against me.

"Fuck me, please, yeah, fuck me like that, Jonas," she screamed.

He slowed for a moment and gestured toward his brother with his chin. "Penn, put your dick in her mouth."

In seconds, Penn was balls deep between Fleur's lips. Her hand reached for his balls, and he held her head for purchase.

Watching her get tag-teamed left me with my own hard dick, so I reached between us and started stroking.

After one particularly hard thrust, Jonas groaned, holding himself deep inside while Fleur continued sucking Penn like a starving animal. Moments later, he hollered, emptying himself in her mouth.

I was minutes away from coming myself, so with my free hand I flipped Fleur onto her knees, ass in the air, and spilled my seed all over her puckered asshole.

Fucking hell.

I called room service and ordered a feast. We were supposed to go to the hotel restaurant but there was no way we were leaving our room now.

CHAPTER 20

DRAKE BANCROFT

I HATED TO DEPART THE NEXT DAY. WE ALL DID. IT had been a short but sweet respite.

And sexy as hell, too.

The beautiful Fleur couldn't get enough of us, and we were all too happy to service her.

I'd never been part of a man-harem before, but it was one of the hottest experiences I'd ever had. Watching her get serviced by the other guys was almost as sexy as going to town on her myself. Our next mini-break could not come soon enough.

But for now, it was time to get back to work. We had important things to do. And to be honest, I was actually looking forward to getting back to the site. The break had been exactly what we'd needed, and everyone's energy buzzed as the Jeep bumped over the dusty roads toward camp.

I felt a surge of adrenaline as we got closer. Everyone quickly unloaded and threw their things in their respective tents. We headed to our site like it was a long-lost friend.

But it immediately became clear that something was off.

"Hmmm. I left my tools right here," Penn said, frowning.

Jonas ran around the periphery of our grid. "What the fuck? Where's the piece of pottery we were digging up?"

I looked over at our neighboring camp. I'd asked them to keep an eye on our things while we were gone.

This was not good. Not at all. And I was getting pissed.

"Um, do you think the looters were back?" Fleur asked with wide eyes. "How'd they know the one night we'd be away?"

Good questions. All good questions.

And no big surprise, Brad was watching us from the next camp. So I waved him over.

Happy for an invite, he hustled in our direction.

"Hi, guys, Fleur," he said, his gaze resting on her a bit longer than it should have.

She reflexively crossed her arms over her chest.

I ran my fingers through my hair. "Um, Brad, someone's been in our campsite."

His eyes got wide. "Really? Is something missing?" he asked with fake-ass incredulity.

"Yeah, Brad, some of our shit is gone," Penn said from between gritted teeth.

"Oh man. That sucks. Majorly."

The lack of concern in his voice said it all. "You know, I did see some folks snooping around over here. I was too busy to come over and see what they were up to, though. Damn. That's a shame," he said, shaking his head.

Seriously?

"So you just let them have a field day here?" I asked.

Penn and Jonas looked like they wanted to take out the asshole themselves.

But Fleur was the one who really laid it down. "Brad. You said you would keep watch while we were gone. But actually, you were not able to and in fact *watched* someone loot our site. Did I get that right?" she asked, getting in his face.

He took a step back. "Um. Well, sorry, but I had my own work to do. You know, we're making some good progress on our site and I can't just drop everything—"

He took another step back, and then another, because Fleur had a finger poking right into his chest.

It actually looked painful.

"Since you're so useless," she said in a raised voice, "why don't you get the fuck out of here!"

"Why don't you take it easy—" he started to say.

But with a firm hand on his shoulder, I turned him in the direction he'd come from. "Fleur's right, Brad. It's best you get back to your own camp now."

He hustled away, but not without throwing a few dirty looks over his shoulder.

Fleur was pale, and distractedly played with the ends of her hair. "I… I'm not comfortable with this looter business. Not at all. We need to do something about this. I'm going to my tent to think this over."

She hobbled away.

"Well, isn't that the shit of it," Penn said.

I couldn't even see straight. "Fleur's idea was a good one. I'll be in my tent for a bit. I need some time."

To cool the fuck off.

Although how I was going to cool off in the desert was beyond me.

CHAPTER 21

FLEUR HOLMES

"Hey, Brad. Thought you weren't supposed to be over here."

He hitched his pants and looked around as if he hadn't already made doubly sure the guys had gone to town before he made his way over.

Sneaky bastard.

And he was in luck. They'd be gone the better part of the day. They'd hesitated for a moment before leaving me alone, but I reminded them I was the one to chase off our last interlopers.

Couldn't argue with that fact.

Besides, and not that I shared this with the guys,

but I had a full can of pepper spray in my pocket ready to take out anyone who threatened our work.

And that included Brad. If I felt threatened, he was fucked.

After he'd been sent packing a couple nights earlier, his regular visits had come to an abrupt halt. But apparently, he hadn't been completely deterred because the moment he saw me alone, he came slithering right over.

He took a long look at my boobs. Because, of course. "So, whatcha working on?" he asked.

Was he kidding? I was digging in the goddamn ground, just like he did all day.

Or was supposed to.

Seriously. The guy spent so much time flapping his gums, I don't know how he got anything done.

"Well, Brad, since our pottery shard findings have gone missing, I'm really hoping to find some more."

He nodded cheerfully. "Well, where there was one, there should be many, right?"

Had this guy really studied archeology?

"So, Fleur, when you coming over for that beer?"

How 'bout never?

"I don't think that's in the cards for me, Brad," I said, turning my attention back to the little area I was carefully dusting. I was pretty sure I was getting close to finding something. Something that I'd hang on to with life and limb. No one else would be stealing anything around here.

Drake had confided in me he believed that over time he'd developed a sixth sense about locating treasures. He'd get a feeling over a certain piece of ground, and more often than not, there'd be something buried there.

I was beginning to feel I might experience the same. I'd been gently removing dirt around a mysterious mound all day, using tiny, precision tools, and something was telling me it was going to pay off at some point.

Hopefully while I was still there.

"You know, Fleur, you should be nicer to me," Brad said.

I looked up from my work, surprised he hadn't taken the hint and split.

"Sorry? What was that?"

He narrowed his eyes at me. "I said, you should be nice to me."

"I am nice to you."

He dropped his head back and laughed. "I said *nicer*." He licked his lips and shifted in his trousers.

Gross.

I discreetly touched the pepper spray in my pocket for confidence.

The man was seriously creeping me out. Like shivers running up my spine creeping me out.

I was tired.

As much as I loved being on the dig with the guys, this stalker dude, coupled with constantly looking over my shoulder for looters, was taking its toll.

They didn't teach us about this stuff in class—the cold, hard vulnerabilities of being in the middle of nowhere, acquiring artifacts that sell for a lot of money on the black market. Both of those things added a layer of danger on top of the excitement of learning about ancient civilizations that took some of the fun out of it.

And I felt that acutely now, with the guys being gone for the afternoon.

Then a hand landed on my shoulder.

I hoped that wasn't Brad. I really did. Because no good was going to come from him touching me.

But it was.

I jumped to my feet and pulled out the pepper spray, pointing it right in his face, my finger on the trigger.

His eyes widened, and he jumped back.

"Touch me again, and you'll get the full effect of what pepper spray has to offer."

"Jesus," he said and turned to hustle back to his own camp.

"Crazy bitch," I heard him mumbling until he was out of our site.

Cripes. I gathered my tools and headed back to the kitchen area, falling into a camp chair and propping up my foot.

Fortunately, my twisted ankle was healing nicely, and while I was still careful about putting weight on it, I didn't much rely on the cane Drake had given me. I wasn't ready to run a marathon, and was still wearing a sneaker with the laces undone, but the improvement was clear.

And I had no one to thank for that more than the guys. They'd taken such good care of me after I hurt myself

In more ways than one.

I looked at my watch and realized they'd be back at any moment. I debated telling them about Brad because I didn't want to start any wars, and I knew they'd be inclined to give him a harsher 'talking to' than he'd already gotten from me.

And that 'talking to' might just include some flying fists.

Just sayin'.

CHAPTER 22

FLEUR HOLMES

"You're really thinking of leaving?"

Drake looked at me like I was crazy.

Maybe I was.

I shrugged. "I don't know, Drake. I am just not sure I feel that safe here. Even with you three guys."

I'd wanted to discuss my concerns and make sure they understood that my reservations about continuing with the dig had nothing to do with them.

But when I thought about it, Drake was essentially my 'boss,' since he'd assigned me the project and was my advisor at school. So I thought it best to bring it up with him first.

MIKA LANE

I was glad I did.

We sat on little camp stools outside his tent.

"Fleur, you started to tell me why you wanted to become an archeologist, but never finished the story."

Ah. The 'story.' It wasn't an easy thing for me to talk about, but Drake's question was legit.

"It's pretty simple, really. My dad used to take my sister and me with him to small digs. You know, looking for fossils, stuff like that. We had boxes of the stuff. I loved it. Then, one day he left for a dig someplace far away—I don't even remember where —and he never came home."

"What do you mean, he never came home?"

I barely ever talked about this. But when I did, my heart started to pound, then to break, just like it did when I was fifteen years old.

"A dirt wall collapsed on him. They tried to dig him out, but by the time they got to them, it was too late."

I hunched slightly forward on my seat, as if that might lessen the tightness in my chest. In the past, I'd get to the point where I could barely breathe. Now, it was just the pain that was debilitating.

"Holy shit. I've heard that story. Your father was Ralph Holmes."

I nodded.

"Jesus, Fleur, I can't believe you never told me that. And that I didn't put two and two together."

He put a hand on my arm. "And I'm sorry you lost your dad, sweetie. He was a really accomplished man."

The coil in my chest unwound a little, enough to let me straighten up in my seat.

I reached for his hand. "I'm sorry I never told you. It's still hard, after all these years, to talk about it. I... I guess I don't want people feeling sorry for me, especially since he was so well-known."

"And that's why you wanted to become an archeologist? I think that's awesome."

Unfinished business and all that.

I looked up to find nothing but understanding in his eyes.

It was funny how just a few short weeks before, Drake had been the imperious Professor Bancroft. He was a good advisor, always supportive, but I'd really not known him at all. And he'd never made an effort to get to know me, either.

How fast things had changed. Although, I was sure they'd go back to the way they were once we were back at the university.

Right?

"Yeah, I guess I always thought if I did the same

work as my dad, it would make me feel closer to him."

"And does it?" he asked.

I took a deep inhale. "Sometimes it does. Sometimes it doesn't."

"So, Fleur. If you're here, doing this work in your father's memory, doesn't it make sense for you to stick this out?" He gestured around us.

I looked back at him, not sure what to say.

"You are safe here. And going forward, the guys and I will make more of an effort to make sure you feel that way. I'd like to ask you to hang on a bit longer. You've made this trip so enjoyable. You're always eager to learn and work, and are clearly willing to be moved out of your comfort zone."

I had to laugh at that one. We both did.

"I love your commitment to the project and how you just dove right in, finding ways to support the excavation."

I looked at our hands, joined between us. "Okay. Okay, I'll stay. But... will you sleep with me tonight?"

I hated to sound like a baby, but I just didn't want to be alone.

A big smile spread across his face, like I'd hoped it would. "Of course. I thought you'd never ask."

I got into my little camp bed to wait for Drake, who had to finish a few things before he joined me.

I relaxed, hands behind my head, feeling pretty good about life. I'd studied hard for so long, first through undergrad, and now in my first year of graduate school. My work was beginning to pay off. I got to take part in my first big dig, and I'd be an important part of the report that followed our efforts.

Maybe even my name would go on it.

And I'd graduated from college punks to real men. Not that our little adventure was going anywhere—I was sure it wasn't—but it taught me that I deserved better than the jerk I'd been dating, and most importantly, that there were better men out there than I'd realized.

What a bonus.

"Hey, darlin,'" Drake said, entering my tent through the zipped door.

I was drowsy after a long day of work and anxiety, and when Drake slipped behind me, both of us on our sides, he wrapped his arms around me. The imperfections of the day began to melt away.

He slid a hand under my sleep T-shirt, his fingers whispering over my tummy, and up my chest until he cupped a breast.

At the same time, his erection pressed against my backside, and he groaned quietly. Pushing his knee between my legs, he pressed against my sex, already throbbing with wild heat and desire. He pressed his lips to my ear for a mind-altering kiss.

Was this all some sort of dream? It sure felt like it.

"Why don't you slide your bottoms down?" he whispered.

All righty then.

I untied the waist of my PJ pants, and slipped one leg out of them. Drake pushed my top leg up with his own, and positioned his hard cock against my wet pussy.

"Guide me," he whispered.

I reached down between my legs, and with a hold on his dick, directed it inside in the most delicious sensation.

He started to rock in and out, with me arching my back to take more of him.

I gripped the edges of my sleeping pad for purchase, and with my orgasm mounting, arched my neck so our faces pressed cheek to cheek. His moans vibrated through me, and we held hands as I came, and then he joined me.

Holy shit, was I in trouble.

CHAPTER 23

PENN KELLER

"What is this? A fucking vacation day?"

I made myself at home in Fleur's tent, where she was still snuggling with Drake from the night before, and tried not to laugh.

I'd heard them going at it, and I was sure my brother had too. I was happy they were having some one-on-one time. Fleur's little sighs, moans, and then orgasmic cries were so sexy I jerked off not once, but two times.

And slept like a baby.

Drake, who I found spooning Fleur when I

barged into her tent, lifted his head from her pillow, squinting against the light flooding in through the tent door, which I'd unzipped all the way and left open.

It was a dick move, but I wanted to torment them a little.

"Close that door up, man, the sun is blinding me," Drake croaked. "C'mon, do it."

"Okay, whiner, give me a sec," I said, and re-zipped the thing closed.

I stood over them, staring down. "She still asleep?"

"Yeah. She is. So why don't you keep your voice down, asshole," Drake hissed.

I had an idea.

"Drake, get out of bed and let me take your place."

"Why?" he moaned.

"Because you have shit to do. Now get up and out of my way," I said.

He groaned quietly, but slipped out of the bed, reaching for his boxers and other clothes.

I, in the meantime, had slipped mine off and crawled in behind Fleur in the exact spot he'd been occupying.

After Drake took off, I buried my nose in the

crook of Fleur's neck, deeply inhaling her sweet scent.

She stirred beneath me and emitted a quiet girl snore.

Fuck, she was cute.

I pressed my lips to her ear lobe, and when she began to stir, reached between her legs where I found her hot and ready.

"Hey, baby," I whispered. "Good morning."

"Mmmm," she murmured, stretching against me.

She twisted just enough to see me, and did a double take, smiling. "You don't look like Drake. What did you do with him?" she whispered, tugging on the bandana around my neck.

I pulled on one of her pretty nipples until she gasped. "He's gone. You'll never see him again."

She flipped over to face me. "Oooh, did you bury him somewhere in the desert?" she giggled.

"I certainly did," I said, brushing my lips across her forehead. "But don't tell anyone, okay?"

She reached down between my legs and grasped my cock.

"Whoa there, baby, not so fast. I don't want to explode all over you before I even get going." I sucked in my breath as the palm of her hand whispered around my cockhead.

"Oh yeah? What are you gonna do if I don't?" she teased.

Fuck, she was killing me.

So, in one swift movement, I flipped her to her back, holding her arms above her head. "You think you can be naughty, little girl?"

Trying to pull out of my grip, she pouted. "Okay, okay. I'll be good."

I stared down at her. "Will I ever get tired of looking at you?"

She gasped and turned bright red. "That's… that's the nicest thing anyone has ever said to me."

Well shit. I hadn't even thought about it. The words had just come flying out of my mouth.

I meant them, though.

When we all got home, she'd get to see Drake and Jonas every day at the university. But I'd be on the other side of town at the museum. Alone.

But it didn't matter. If she was open to it, I'd find a way to see her as often as she could stand me. Which, hopefully, would be a lot.

I moved between her parted thighs so that my cock bounced against her, and slid up and down between her juicy pussy lips.

"Ahhhh…" she moaned, her eyes closing as her head dropped back onto her pillow.

I ground against her like that until I nearly had her coming. "Baby, are you ready? Are you ready for my cock?" I rasped.

"Oh god yes, Penn, please," she mumbled.

I shifted my hips and aimed my dick at her opening, then rammed her as deeply as I could.

She started to buck under me, and her moans grew louder and louder.

"Fuck me, baby, just like that, Penn," she cried.

She shuddered under me as I brought her to orgasm again, and then, just before I came, I pulled out and spurted all over her stomach.

I bent to kiss her as she continued to convulse under me.

"Want to hear something funny?" I asked her after a while.

She slowly opened her eyes. "Of course."

I flopped over on my side, supporting myself on an elbow. "When we first arrived here, Drake was going on and on about how a romance brings a curse to a dig. He was pretty serious about it."

I shook my head with a chuckle.

"Isn't that how he met his wife?" Fleur asked.

"Yeah. As far as I know."

"Well. Do you think I've proved him wrong?" she asked, her eyes twinkling.

"If he hasn't changed his mind yet, I am sure he will soon."

"YOU'LL NEVER BELIEVE THIS."

My brother and I turned to Drake, having helped ourselves to giant mugs of coffee. We needed to ingest the addictive stuff before the day got too hot to drink it.

I sincerely hoped Drake hadn't found anything else missing from our site. As it was, the loss of the pottery shards was devastating enough. Although, I was pretty sure he had a plan for getting them back.

He was no dummy. He'd been attending digs for many years, and had a good grasp on how things worked.

And how to deal with looters.

I glanced around for Fleur, who was already hard at work doing the delicate task of brushing sand away from something that might turn out to be a significant finding.

Her patience floored me. She could sit for hours, gently coaxing something magical out of the ground as if she'd always known it was there. Some people in archeology just had a knack that way.

But she floored me in other ways, too. There she

was in her dusty khaki shorts, tank top, and wide brimmed hat to protect that freckled skin, her long red hair gathered into a braid that fell in front of her left shoulder. She kept pushing it behind her back and out of the way of her work, and it kept falling right back in front.

In short, she was adorable and beautiful at the same time.

I'd had no idea a woman could pull that off. But she did, in spades.

"Hey. Earth to Penn," my brother said, nudging me in the ribs.

"Oh. Shit. Sorry guys. Guess I got a little distracted."

Drake and Jonas smiled. We were clearly all in the same boat.

"What were you saying, Drake?"

"Penn, he was telling us that Brad, the fucker from the next camp over—"

"I know who that asshole is," I interrupted.

My brother nodded. "Apparently, our neighbor managed to get photos of us with the lovely Fleur, and now he wants in on our findings."

Wait. What?

How the hell did that happen?

And when could I pound him into the ground?

Drake pressed his lips together in a thin line. "He's also extorting money from me."

My head snapped in Drake's direction. "What? Why is he hitting *you* up?"

Drake looked at Jonas.

Did they know something I didn't?

"Penn," Jonas started to say, "Drake comes from— how can I say this without sounding tacky as fuck?— he comes from a family of means."

I looked at Drake, who nodded silently.

Okay. That was cool. Drake had money. That was why he sprang for the fancy hotel we went to with Fleur.

"Is this… like a big secret or something?" I asked. "That you have money or something?"

Drake shrugged. "I keep things like this private. My grandfather was one of the early Wall Street financiers, so it's all inherited. It's not like I earned it. Anyway, I'm not going to flaunt my family money around the university. People would look at me in a different light. Money is fucked up that way."

So, Drake was a secret billionaire. Holy fuck.

But regardless, what Brad was doing, or trying to do, was bullshit.

"You know, I could just walk over there and pummel the shit out of him," I offered.

Jonas raised his eyebrows at me. He knew I was good for it.

Drake laughed. "Tempting as that may be, his profound interest in what we're doing has got me suspicious."

"Yeah? How so?" I asked, trying to relax my clenched fists.

I was itching to teach that punk a lesson.

"I… I just have some theories I want to work through. I hadn't even been sure whether to share this with you guys, and I definitely don't want to tell Fleur yet. But you're all involved now so you deserve to know."

"How the hell did he get photos of us with Fleur?" Jonas asked.

"He must have hired someone to take photos of our little getaway, by our supposedly 'private' pool. The hotel and their 'security' will be hearing from me about this. But first things first."

Holy shit.

"When he initially came to me, I nearly told him to pound sand. But I may have a better approach. Please just be patient with me for a day or two."

I looked over at Fleur, working her ass off in the dirt. She looked over our way and caught us all looking at her. She smiled and waved and got back to work.

I was fucking pissed. It was one thing for someone to mess with me and the guys, but dragging Fleur into this, especially when she was just starting her career, made me see red.

I really hoped Drake's plan to address this bullshit was a solid one.

Otherwise, our little friend Brad would be meeting with my solid fist.

CHAPTER 24

FLEUR HOLMES

"Hey, guys. What's the pow-wow all about?"

If I weren't mistaken, they were avoiding my gaze.

What the hell was going on?

I'd been working from sunup to sundown on what I hoped would be a good find. I wanted to contribute to the success of the dig, and share that with the guys. I could see it now... a well-reviewed article about our finds, with all four of our names on the front cover.

It would be so amazing.

But to make that happen, I couldn't stop working. I only had so much time out here in the desert and had to make every moment count.

Well, except for those when I was naked with the guys. That was a different sort of priority.

They all glanced down at me, where I was working in our little pit. They'd been talking for a long time in the mess tent, and hopefully were thinking it was time to get to work.

What had they been talking about so seriously, anyway? I'd considered joining them to see what was up, but figured I'd catch up later.

"Oh, just some planning. That sort of thing," Drake said quickly.

Okay…

"What's that you have there," Jonas asked, crouching for a better view.

"I believe this is a…" I said, working my tools around the edges of the artifact as gently as I could.

But I couldn't finish. I didn't want to jinx myself by wondering out loud if I'd found what I'd hoped I had—a fully intact clay pot.

It would be incredible to find something like this that hadn't been damaged by the passage of time, but even more so if it indicated there was an entire treasure trove left behind by some ancient civilization just a few feet further below the surface.

This was the sort of things archeologists dreamt of.

And I was pretty sure I'd found what I'd been dreaming of.

They stared where I was still brushing away loose earth, their eyes wide.

Yup, they were thinking the same thing I was.

This was going to be fucking massive.

"You know, Fleur, I was about to tell you to stop working so damn hard, but I can see that would have been a mistake—"

Before Drake had even finished, I gingerly lifted the pot, careful not to let it slip between the fingers of my soft cotton gloves, and balancing it in the open palms of my hands.

"Holy shit. Look at that," Penn said.

"Jesus," Jonas yelled, "you know what you've done, Fleur? This is fucking massive."

"Hold it right there," Drake said, taking one photo after another of the pot from different angles.

I couldn't believe our find, and I couldn't believe I was the one who'd uncovered it. It could have been any of us, for sure, but this would cement my role as part of the team.

Some might say it was beginner's luck, but I hadn't been digging for hours every day for my freaking health. I *knew* there was something here. I just knew it.

I put the pot into Drake's outstretched hands, and Penn reached to help me out of the pit. As soon as I was on my feet, he picked me up and twirled me around.

"Woo-hoo!" he screamed. "This is better than finding gold."

He kissed me squarely on the lips before his brother elbowed him out of the way to do the same.

Oh my god. How did I get so lucky?

Drake stared at the little pot in his hands. "This is freaking awesome, Fleur."

I put my hands on my hips. I had something important to say and I wanted the guys to pay attention. "From here on in, we need to have a night watch over our site. I'll take the first night, and you guys can figure out who goes after that."

They looked at me like I was crazy.

"Um, good idea about putting together a night patrol, but there's no way you're doing something like that alone, Fleur," Jonas said.

I already had an answer for this. I was prepared.

"All right. Fine. If I even smell any sort of trouble, I *promise* to get one of you guys. I won't confront anyone on my own like I did that other time."

Even though pepper spray had a permanent

home in my pocket, it probably made sense to call for backup, should it ever be needed. But I wasn't going to sit out a night shift. I hadn't shied away from any of the hard work on this dig, and I wasn't starting now.

They looked at each other, and Drake slowly nodded. "I can work with that. But no heroics Fleur. All our hard work will have gone to shit if anything happens to you."

It was settled.

CHAPTER 25

FLEUR HOLMES

TURNS OUT STAYING UP ALL NIGHT TO WATCH AN excavation site was about as exciting as watching paint dry. The desert night was beautiful, without a doubt, but it was dead silent, and I couldn't see more than ten feet in any direction, even with my head-lamp turned up high.

Simply put, there was nothing to do but stare into the blackness and hope the thugs had decided to stay home that night. And every time I started to read my book, I began to doze off.

I wandered back to the mess tent to make myself

some coffee and to my horror, found there wasn't enough left to even make one pot.

Goddammit. How was I supposed to stay up now? And hadn't the guys just gone shopping for provisions? How could they have forgotten coffee?

There was no way I could stay awake now, and while it might not hurt to doze off a bit, hadn't I pressured the guys to let me pull my weight? Slacking was not an option.

I peered over at the neighboring camp, one we'd tried to stay away from since our run-in with Brad. Not surprisingly, people over there were wide awake. It seemed like that group was more into partying than anything else.

Did I dare head over?

Oh, what the fuck. I needed to stay awake, and to stay awake, I needed coffee.

Grabbing my empty mug, I turned off my head-lamp and quietly walked toward the campsite so that if I decided to bail at the last minute, I could.

As I got nearer, I could see a few members of the team sitting around a table, playing a card game. A couple were drinking beer, but I saw someone with a cup of coffee.

I was in luck.

Yes.

"Hey, what's up, bro? I got some good news for you."

I whipped around, almost doing a three-hundred-sixty-degree spin to see where the voice had come from, and whether it had been talking to me.

"Yeah, it's the fucking middle of the night here. It's the only time I can call you. Most of the camp is asleep and the couple folks who are up don't give a shit what I do."

That was Brad's voice.

I inched closer to their latrine, where the voice was coming from, and realized Brad was on the camp's satphone, probably thinking he could have a conversation from there without anyone over-hearing.

"Yeah, I was able to get my hands on some of the shit the idiots in the next camp over dug up. Nah, they'll never know. And the shit they've come up with will demand a fortune on the black market. We're gonna be rich motherfuckers."

What the fucking fuck?

Brad had stolen our stuff? When he was supposed to be watching it? And then had blamed it on local looters?

A wave of dizziness washed over me, and I prayed I wouldn't fall over and reveal myself. I clamped my hand over my mouth so not even my breathing could be heard.

"They have no fucking idea," he continued.

Ohmygod, ohmygod, ohmygod.

"So listen. They have the girl guarding the site tonight. Yeah, I know, how fucking dumb is that. I'm having the guys from the village come and pretend to be there to fuck their stuff up to throw them off my trail. It will be easy. They don't have a damn clue."

He was silent for a moment

I no longer needed coffee and in fact was exploding with adrenaline. I wanted to tear him limb from limb.

"Yeah, I told them to just take the girl. She's a stuck-up bitch. Maybe they can teach her a lesson."

He burst out laughing and ended his call.

I flattened myself against the latrine while he headed back to his camp. In the light from the mess tent, Brad silently returned the satphone to its proper spot and noisily joined the rest of the people playing cards.

For several moments, I couldn't move, I was so petrified. But then I quietly jogged back to my own camp, a million thoughts racing through my head.

But there was one thing I was sure of. It was time to wake up the guys.

CHAPTER 26

JONAS KELLER

"You should have let me take that little fucker the first time I mentioned it."

Penn was bouncing in his shoes, ready to kill someone. But Drake had managed to calm him, at least for the time being. He sure as hell wasn't about to listen to me.

I didn't blame him for his testosterone overload. I was pretty fucking pissed, myself. All I could say was that our plan had better work. We were using our lovely girl Fleur as bait, for Christ's sake.

Which I was not at all convinced was a good idea. In fact I thought it was a pretty fucking risky one.

But the options were few if we wanted to trip up our confirmed nemesis, Brad.

Not that it would be hard to trip him up.

The man might have been duplicitous but that didn't mean he was smart.

And it looked like the trap we'd set for him was one he was about to walk right into.

I peered around the corner of the mess tent from where the guys and I were hiding in the shadows, to where Fleur was sitting on full display, like a shiny lure on the end of a fishing line. As far as I was concerned, she should have just had a sign over her head reading *come and get me.*

She was doing her best to appear calm and collected, pretending to read a book, but by now I knew her well enough to realize she was anything but.

Especially since every now and then she would, without moving her head, shift her gaze around to see if there was anything or anyone coming at her.

Couldn't blame her, since we *knew* someone was coming after her, not to mention the site's artifacts.

Of course, the dig's findings were of little concern when our girl was putting her well-being on the line.

I forced myself to remember to breathe, that's

how tightly wound I was. All I could think was that if anybody were to lay a finger on her, they'd be lucky they didn't end up six feet under. And that it would be a race between my brother and me to see who could get to them first.

Drake, Penn, and I were ready. And, Drake had his gun loaded.

Regardless of our planning, there were still a myriad of things that could go wrong, and because of that, I wasn't completely comfortable having Fleur front and center. But if she weren't the sitting duck Brad's contacts had been told to expect, no part of our plan would ever work.

We'd just be back at square one.

What had incensed me more than anything—even more than having our artifacts or tools stolen—was Brad's cavalier attitude about Fleur, and how he'd told his lackeys to just take her away, whatever the fuck that meant.

If there were any one reason to pound his skull in, I'd say this was the best.

From our hiding spot in the dark, I glanced over to Brad's camp. If my eyes weren't playing tricks on me, he was hanging with a couple of the all-night card players, but continually craning his neck in our direction to see Fleur waiting like a sitting duck.

I whipped in the direction of the pitch-black night, distracted by a small sound coming from well beyond the reach of the light Fleur was pretending to read under.

And it was clear she'd heard it, too, because, while she didn't look up from the pages of her book, she stiffened. Someone who didn't know her might not realize it, but to me, her body was coiled to the point of being painful.

The sound got closer, and then there were quiet voices near our pit.

Just as we'd planned, Fleur called out into the darkness. "Hello? Is someone out there?"

The noise stopped for a few seconds, then continued.

Whoever the intruders were, they didn't answer, knowing she'd have to venture into the darkness to see who it was and what they were doing.

She spoke a little louder the second time. "I said, who's out there? You shouldn't be here. I'm going to call the authorities."

Still nothing.

Little did they know, the authorities were already on their way.

"I'm warning you, I... I have a weapon," she lied as she inched into the darkness.

I'd never felt my body so wound with tension.

My girl—I mean, *our* girl—was putting her life on the line for the sake of our work.

I was blown away by her courage. I'm not sure I would so willingly walk into such a trap, even if I knew I had the backup of three big, pissed-off guys like us, as well as the authorities drawing near.

My fears became a reality when I heard Fleur scream. But seconds later, as if on cue, floodlights turned our camp into broad daylight as the local gendarmerie jumped into action, guns drawn, hollering in a local dialect I couldn't understand.

With the area lit up, I watched Fleur turn to one of the guys. He'd made the fatal mistake of getting too close to her, which earned him a kick in the balls with her heavy boot. Grunting, he fell forward. She turned to the other guy, who started running.

Right into the arms of a cop.

The would-be thieves and kidnappers, admitting defeat, threw their arms into the air, yelling and pointing in the direction of the neighboring camp. I turned and saw Brad watching the whole scene with his mouth hanging open. And before the fool knew what was happening, Drake was behind him, grabbing him in a chokehold.

Not being much of a morning person, I usually missed sunrise. But because the local cops had just carted off Brad and his accomplices, I was wide awake for this one.

While the morning was still cool from the desert night temperatures, the warm sun coming up over the sandy horizon was a peaceful contrast to the night before of danger, intrigue, and even betrayal.

As we'd suspected—like I said, Brad wasn't too bright—he'd hired some local guys to take the attention off him when he was the looter all along. The leader of his dig, also his boss, went through his stuff and found not only what he'd stolen from us, but also things he'd stolen from his own camp. And he'd been discovered just in time. Brad was just days away from leaving and dumping his loot on the black market to make his fortune. Neither he, nor the items he'd stolen, would have ever been seen again.

What if we hadn't caught him? What if Fleur hadn't lucked out and overheard his plans? Our artifacts might have been gone, but what would have happened to our girl?

I didn't even want to think about it.

I felt for the guys Brad had hired. They were no masterminds. They were just trying to make a little extra money to feed their families. The real criminals in all this were the Brads of the world and the greedy fuckers who thought it was okay to purchase and own stolen artifacts, who thought it okay to build personal collections of things that really ought to be enjoyed by everyone.

"I say we don't work today," Drake said, stretching and yawning.

"Cheers to that," Penn agreed.

Fleur, who was more alert than any of us, yet who'd actually been awake the longest, put her hands on her hips. "I have an idea," she teased.

Fuck, I hoped it was the same thing I was thinking.

"Meet you guys in my tent?" she said, sashaying in the direction of her little 'love shack,' as my brother called it.

"Be there in a minute," Penn called after her, looking happy as a pig in shit. "Goddamn she's cute."

"What are we gonna do about it?" Drake asked.

Penn shrugged. "We'll all date her."

Drake looked at him like he was crazy, but most likely hoped he wasn't.

"Jonas and I have shared a woman before. It was hot as shit."

"Penn, that was a little different. I mean, she was nice and all, but what we have with Fleur is something... special."

Shit, even calling it *special* seemed to diminish it.

"Well, we've told her we liked her. Now it's time to have a more pointed discussion," Drake said.

He was right. But there were more fun things to attend to, first.

CHAPTER 27

FLEUR HOLMES

I COULD BARELY KEEP MY EYES OPEN.

But I wasn't going to sleep, not yet.

The guys filtered in to find me reclining on my camp mattress, naked, with my hair streaming over a pillow.

"Fuck me," Jonas growled as he started toward me.

"Wait," I said, holding my hand like a *stop* sign.

The guys looked at each other.

"Huh?" Jonas said.

I lay back, running my hands over my heated skin, and stopping at my breasts. I pulled on my nipples until the guys' mouths dropped open, then continued to my stomach, until I reached my legs, which I slowly spread open.

"Holy fuck," Drake breathed.

I circled a finger around my hard clit, then ran it through my wet folds, pulling myself open just enough to give the guys a show.

"Mmmm," I moaned. "Feels so nice."

"Keep going, baby," Penn whispered.

I glanced at him long enough to watch him whip out his cock. In two long strokes, it was swollen and stiff, dripping with a glistening drop of precum.

My fingers wandered to my opening, where I pushed one inside, followed by another.

"Look at our girl," Jonas rasped, "fucking herself."

Drake took another step toward me. "Baby, I gotta have some of that," he demanded.

I looked at him, his face covered in painful desire.

I wanted him, too. I wanted all of them.

But first I had to torment them a little.

"Okay, Drake. Come over here," I beckoned with my free hand.

He stood over me.

"Take out your cock."

He whipped that thing out of his pants in record time.

"Now come down here and fuck my face."

I lay on my back as he positioned himself, a knee on either side of my head. I guided him just past my lips to tease him a little, tasting the delicious precum dripping from his cock.

But before I really began to devour him, I waved over the twins.

"You," I said, pointing at Penn, "put your cock in my hand right here, and you, Jonas, fuck my pussy."

They smiled broadly.

I took Drake as deeply as I could. He pulled back out, almost all the way, then rammed his cock down my throat again with a thrust of his hips.

At the same time, Jonas snapped on a condom and positioned himself at my opening.

"You ready, baby?" he asked.

With my mouth full, I couldn't say anything, so I just nodded.

With Penn sliding in and out of my grip, my mouth full of Drake, and my pussy full of Jonas, I was in heaven. I was pleasing all my guys—

Shit. Did I just say *my guys*?

—and they were pleasing me.

Well, more than pleasing me. It was like I'd died and gone to heaven.

Drake pulled out of my mouth just in time to come all over my tits, which left me free to scream from the fucking Jonas was giving me.

His thrusts were rocking me, bringing me close, and then backing off again. I'd never been teased like that.

In one swift movement, he flipped me over so I was on top, straddling him.

I got to work, grinding my pussy on him when either Drake or Penn—I wasn't sure who, and I didn't care—started to run a wet finger back... there.

Holy shit.

I'd never explored backdoor play and wasn't sure I wanted to, but the sensation of a finger gently tickling me there was... kind of cool.

In fact, it was more than cool. I fucking loved it, and while riding Jonas's cock, wagged my ass for more.

A moment later, a fingertip was pressing inside me, and I almost screamed stop, but when it got further inside, it actually felt good. Like it was meant to be there.

Combined with the sensation of a full pussy, it was enough to drive a person crazy.

It turned out having both my ass and pussy serviced was pretty fucking awesome. Head bucking, tits bouncing, and hair flying all over the place, I exploded in orgasm, one after the other, convulsing from the overload of sensation.

Grabbing my hips, Jonas thrust his hips upward

one more time, grinding his teeth, followed by an ear-splitting bellow.

When he finally released me, I fell forward on him, dripping in sweat, weak, and shaky, as if everything I was had been taken out of me and enjoyed by my three lovers.

I didn't want anything to change. I wanted to stay here forever with the guys, living just as we were, digging by day and making love by night.

That wasn't too much to ask, was it?

CHAPTER 28

FLEUR HOLMES

T<small>URNED OUT THAT WAS ENTIRELY TOO MUCH TO ASK</small> because when we all woke up, mid-day, Drake reminded us a new crew would be arriving the next day, and that some of us had to double up on our accommodations. Our little love fest was coming to a screeching halt.

But maybe it was for the best?

How the hell would I explain what I was doing with three guys? Even my open-minded sister would have a hard time with that one.

I looked around my tent and sighed. In the weeks

I'd been at the camp, I'd let my shit spread out all over the place. But now that I was sharing with another woman, it was time to get my act in gear and tidy up.

Or should I just pack up and get out while things were going well?

Maybe it was time for me to head home. I'd done good work, having been the one to find the most important artifact the group had found in years. That was a pretty good track record, especially for one's first major dig.

I had no complaints.

While I wouldn't mind staying longer, there wasn't much left for me to do. And with the arrival of new folks, the little fling between me and the guys had to come to an end, too.

"Hello," a female voice called.

Crap. It had been ages since I'd heard another woman's voice.

I pushed the tent flaps open. "Hey. Come on in. I'm Fleur."

My new roommate looked around the tent at all my luggage and set her backpack down in a corner, then looked me up and down.

Jesus. Even more reason to get the hell out.

She approached me, hands on hips. "So, I heard

you had some pretty awesome discoveries. What did you find?" she asked, like she was testing me.

I so wasn't in the mood.

I shrugged. "Drake will brief you."

And I went back to packing my shit.

CHAPTER 29

DRAKE BANCROFT

"Fleur? Hey, Fleur, you up yet?"

There was rustling from inside her tent, and the door flaps unzipped and flew open. There she stood, surrounded by her mountain of suitcases, dressed a little more appropriately than she had been the day she'd arrived.

Seemed like a year ago, not just weeks.

In her jeans and sneakers, she was her usual gorgeous self, but there was a new confidence about her.

And a new sexiness, too.

Fuck, I was going to miss her.

She'd come to me the night before, explaining that her work here was done, and that she needed to get back.

"What about us?" I'd asked.

"What do you mean, *us*?"

I gestured toward Penn and Jonas. "All of us. The three of us."

Avoiding my gaze, she looked down. "I... I don't know."

"But we want to be with you," I'd said.

She finally looked up at me. "I know. And I want to be with all of you, too. But how? How would we make that work?"

I didn't have an answer.

But I did have an idea. I just didn't want to show my cards before it was a sure thing.

"I remember these suitcases," I said, reaching inside her tent the next morning at the crack of dawn.

Careful not to disturb her sleeping roommate, Jonas and Penn, right behind me, grabbed the last two bags, and Fleur followed us to the Jeep.

I opened the back of it and started loading her things.

"What's all this stuff?" she asked, pointing at someone else's luggage.

Penn and Jonas smiled at each other.

"Darlin'," I started, "you didn't think you were getting rid of us that easily, did you?"

She looked from one of us to the other. "Huh?"

We'd truly confused her. Which we'd hoped we would. Makes for a better surprise and all.

"That's our stuff, Fleur," Penn said, throwing an arm around her shoulders.

Now she looked even more confused. "Wait. I thought you all were staying."

I grabbed my own duffle, which I'd hidden out of sight, from the other side of the Jeep and threw it in on top of Fleur's things.

"We got some good news for ya, baby," Jonas said.

"Um, okay. What's the good news?"

We looked at Drake. He'd made the arrangements, so he could share them.

I adjusted my sunglasses. It was going to be good to get out of the worst of the heat. Not that we were going to be completely done with it.

"I made a couple calls, Fleur. Thanks to your great find, the museum and the university are putting together a traveling exhibit as soon as the dig is complete. All four of us will accompany the artifacts and be on several speaking panels as we travel around the world. All expenses are paid, and it will look great on the resume of a new archeologist. You can work on your thesis while we travel."

Her mouth dropped open, but nothing came out, then it opened again, like a fish gasping for air.

"What do you say?" I asked. "You want to join us?"

"We know you were really dying to go home. So this might not be your thing," Jonas teased. "I'm sure the department misses you."

Penn smiled at her, pretending to be cheery. But I knew what he was really hoping for. "If you decide not to come, we'll understand. But word has it we'll be at the best hotels and be wined and dined by all the movers and shakers in our field."

"Wha... what..." she mumbled.

Jesus. I knew she'd be surprised but I never thought she'd be *this* surprised.

It was part of what I loved about her. No sense of entitlement. Just pure, unadulterated modesty.

And, yeah, I did say *love*.

She finally got her voice back. "Are you sure? I can come?"

The three of us guys burst out laughing.

"What do you mean, can you come," Penn asked, throwing his arms around her.

He clearly didn't give a shit about who might be watching.

"Um, well, I mean…" she stammered.

"Darlin', there'd be no trip without you," I said.

A slow smile spread across her face. "Well then, of course I'll come."

Penn whirled her around and when he was done, Jonas did the same.

But I pulled Fleur to me and laid a big kiss on her, something I'd been dying to do all morning.

Actually, I'd been dying to do that for a lot longer than just this morning, and I could say the wait was definitely worth it.

Did you like *Her Dirty Archeologists*? Learn about the next book in the Men at Work series,
Her Dirty Mechanics

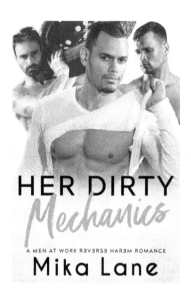

HER DIRTY
Mechanics

A MEN AT WORK R3V3RS3 HAR3M ROMANCE

Mika Lane

The sexy mechanics at my father's car repair shop get all kinds of motors running. And they're more than willing to teach me how to handle a stick...or two or three.

When I move back to my home town to run my dad's car repair shop, it looks like his hunky mechanics are going to be running...me.

One is my brother's best friend.

Another, the boy I skinny-dipped with when I was sixteen.

And last but not least, a scary ex-con.

All three drive very...fast.

And are talented with their...tools.

While giving me a hard...ride.

They're teaching me all I need to know.

And I don't mean just about fixing cars.
Life in the fast lane is so much fun with the right mechanics by your side.

Download it now: *Her Dirty Mechanics*

and... find all Mika Lane books here

GET A FREE SHORT STORY
Join my Insider Group
Exclusive access to private release specials, giveaways, the opportunity to receive advance reader copies (ARCs), and other random musings.

ABOUT THE AUTHOR

Dear Reader:

Please join my Insider Group and be the first to hear about giveaways, sales, pre-orders, ARCs, and most importantly, a free sexy short story: http://mikalane.com/join-mailing-list/.

Writing has been a passion of mine since, well, forever (my first book was "The Day I Ate the Milky-way," a true fourth-grade masterpiece). These days, steamy romance, both dark and funny, gives purpose to my days and nights as I create worlds and characters who defy the imagination. I live in magical Northern California with my own handsome alpha dude, sometimes known as Mr. Mika Lane, and an evil cat named Bill. These two males also defy my imagination from time to time.

A lover of shiny things, I've been known to try to new recipes on unsuspecting friends, find hiding places so I can read undisturbed, and spend my last dollar on a plane ticket somewhere.

I have several books for you to choose from including perennially favorite Billionaire and Reverse Harem romances. And have you see my Player Series about male escorts who make the ladies of Hollywood curl their toes and forget their names? Hottttt.... And my Anti-hero/Mafia books are now out in audio.

Check out my latest series, The Men at Work Collection, about hot men and the professions that make them successful masters of the universe... and the women they love.

I'll always promise you a hot, sexy romp with kick-ass but imperfect heroines, and some version of a modern-day happily ever after.

I LOVE to hear from readers when I'm not dreaming up naughty tales to share. Join my Insider Group so we can get to know each other better http://mikalane.com/join-mailing-list, or contact me here: https://mikalane.com/contact.

xoxo

Love,
Mika